Birthday Cake and Bodies

A Peridale Cafe MYSTERY

AGATHA FROST

For questions and comments about this book, please contact
pinktreepublishing@gmail.com

www.pinktreepublishing.com
www.agathafrost.com

Edited by Keri Lierman and Karen Sellers

ISBN: 9781549961151
Imprint: Independently published

ALSO BY AGATHA FROST

The Scarlet Cove Series
Dead in the Water
Castle on the Hill

The Peridale Café Series
Pancakes and Corpses
Lemonade and Lies
Doughnuts and Deception
Chocolate Cake and Chaos
Shortbread and Sorrow
Espresso and Evil
Macarons and Mayhem
Fruit Cake and Fear
Birthday Cake and Bodies
Gingerbread and Ghosts

A

Peridale Cafe
MYSTERY

Book Nine

CHAPTER 1

Julia hated lying. There had not been a day in the last two weeks where she had not lied to Barker. Some of them had been white lies that had easily rolled off her tongue, and others had been big and complicated lies that had stuck in her throat and made her feel sick. What she hated more than the constant lying was how good she was at it.

Standing on the edge of the platform, Julia checked her watch for the third time that minute.

She looked up and down Peridale's tiny train station, the murky early November sky swirling above. She was glad the station was completely deserted. The last thing she wanted was for one of Peridale's gossips to spot her. Even the least juicy titbits of information had a way of spreading around the village like a forest fire in the height of summer. It would start with *'guess who I saw waiting for a train? Julia South! I thought she drove?'* which would somehow find its way to Barker within the hour. She would not usually mind being the subject of idle village gossip, except Barker thought she was clothes shopping with Jessie in Oxford. It was a simple lie that had been necessary, and one she knew Barker would not question. There had been no way he would have wanted to spend his Sunday afternoon shopping with two women, and he would not notice that they were lacking shopping bags when they returned later in the evening. Even if he did notice, a simple *'we didn't find anything we liked'* would put an end to it, and they would eat dinner none the wiser. Another day, another set of lies.

"The train is running two minutes late," Jessie called from the small ticket office, her voice echoing off the cream and emerald green tiles, which had not been changed since the station's opening in 1891.

"When are they ever on time?"

Julia's seventeen-year-old foster daughter joined her on the platform edge, kicking a drink can onto the tracks with the tip of her Doc Martens. She peered from under her low hood, her eyes tired and red. Jessie would not admit it, but she had been crying again.

"It will get easier," Julia assured her, squeezing Jessie's shoulder firmly. "The first heartbreak is always the hardest."

"I'm not heartbroken," Jessie mumbled, shrugging off Julia's hand. "I dumped him."

Julia nodded her understanding as Jessie sat down on the green wrought-iron bench under the hand-painted '*Platform Two - This Way*' sign. Even though Jessie had been the one to formally end things with Billy Matthews, the boy she had been seeing for the last couple of months, it had been Billy's decision to suddenly enlist in the army. Julia sympathised with Jessie, but she could not blame Billy for wanting to leave the village. There were not many opportunities for boys like him in Peridale, especially ones who had been raised on the Fern Moore Estate.

It had been a couple of weeks since Jessie had agreed to let Julia officially adopt her, and nine months since Julia had taken Jessie in off the streets after catching her stealing cakes from her café. In that time, Julia and Jessie's bond was as close to mother and daughter as it could be, but it did not mean Julia had all of the answers when it came to dealing with teenage heartbreak. She was trying to be there for Jessie as much as she could, but Jessie was not the type of girl who willingly showed her emotions.

The shrill scream of metal on metal pierced through the cold air, signalling the approaching train. Julia looked into the tunnel, the yellowy headlights illuminating the darkness.

"They're here," she said, almost to herself. "It's really happening."

Nerves bubbled over in her stomach, a culmination of the last two weeks of meticulous planning. She almost could not believe she had somehow pulled it together.

Jessie stuffed her mobile phone into her pocket to join Julia by the edge of the platform as the train screeched to a halt in front of them. A robotic female voice announced the arrival of the train, as well as the rest of the stations it would stop at before it reached its final destination of Bath. Julia looked at Jessie, an anxious smile shaking her lips. Jessie did not even attempt to return it.

The electronic doors shuddered open, snapping into place against the metal shell of the train. Burnt oil mixed with Julia's nerves, further turning her stomach. She stepped back, suddenly realising she did not even know what they looked like.

An attractive woman with straight, strawberry blonde hair stepped onto the platform, a designer weekend bag over her shoulder. She was wearing a pale cream trench coat, figure-hugging black jeans, and heels to match. Julia would have put her in her early forties. A similarly aged bald man with dazzling blue eyes followed the woman, his thin nose bent to the left of his slender face. He was wearing a leather jacket over a blue polo shirt buttoned up to the neck, paired with stylish, fitted pale blue jeans, and he too was carrying a designer weekend bag. A younger man in a shirt and tie, who appeared to be in his early-twenties jumped off next, with his own weekend bag. He seemed to be a direct genetic result of the man and the woman. He was tall and slender with a thin nose, and he had coiffed strawberry blond hair, which was receding at the temples. The man and woman looked around the station with mild curiosity, but the young man did not bother looking up from his phone. The three of them had naturally tanned skin, hinting at several tropical holidays a year. Julia waited for someone else to get off the train, almost certain the attractive family was not who she had been anxiously waiting for. A whistle pierced the air, causing the doors to shudder back into place. The train eased out of the station, leaving the trio behind.

"Julia?" the man with the crooked nose asked, his voice belonging to that of the man she had spoken to that morning on the telephone. "Julia South?"

"Yes," she said, suddenly smiling at the new arrivals. "Sorry! I was expecting someone who looked like Barker. Ethan, isn't it?"

"That's right," the man dropped his bag to shake Julia's hand. "Don't worry, none of us look alike. We all have different fathers. Well, except Theo and me."

"Oh," Julia said, trying to hide how little Barker had told her about his family. "And you must be Ethan's wife?"

"It's so lovely to meet you," the woman said, her voice soft and soothing, reminding Julia of a radio presenter her gran listened to in the afternoons. "I'm Dawn. You're so pretty! Is your dress vintage?"

"It is," Julia said, blushing as she looked down at

her 1940s yellow and pink polka-dot dress. "I think I should have opted for something a little warmer."

"Don't be silly!" Dawn cried, winking at Julia with a playful grin. "Style doesn't care about the weather."

Julia did not admit her love for vintage fashion came from the way her mother used to dress and less about making a fashion statement.

"This must be your daughter?" Ethan asked, suddenly turning to Jessie. "It's nice to meet you."

"*Foster* daughter," Jessie corrected him bluntly, accepting the man's handshake weakly.

"We're in the process of adoption," Julia added, apologising for Jessie's abruptness with a smile. "It takes a while. How was your journey?"

"I can't get a *signal!*" the young man cried, pointing his phone up to the sky, ignoring Julia's question. "I only have *one* bar!"

"This is our son, Luke," Ethan said, slapping the boy on the shoulder as Luke stared at his phone. "Forgive him. He thinks he'll die if his emails don't refresh once a minute."

"It's for business, Dad," the boy snapped, skipping the introductions. "Is there Wi-Fi where we're staying?"

"I think so," Julia replied uncertainly. "You'll be

staying with my dad and his wife at Peridale Manor. I did try to get you into the B&B, but Evelyn closes up every winter. She's travelling around New Zealand with her grandson. She didn't even know she had a grandson until last month. Her daughter died and – it's a long story."

Ethan and Dawn stared blankly at her with polite smiles. Julia had to remind herself the local village news would be of little interest to these city folk.

"I should have called ahead about Luke joining us," Ethan said apologetically. "It was a last minute decision."

"I didn't even *want* to come," Luke mumbled like a boy half his age would. "I had to cancel important meetings for this."

"Like I said, you haven't seen your Uncle Barker since Bethany's funeral, and you can do the meetings on video-link," Dawn said, clearly exasperated by her son. "It's been three years. Family is important."

"When it suits you," Luke muttered, before cramming his phone into his pocket and turning to his father. "Is my cousin coming?"

"Bella?" Ethan asked, turning to Julia. "I don't know. Did Theo even agree to come?"

Theo, another of Barker's brothers, had been the

most difficult to pin down. When Julia had decided she was going to plan a surprise birthday party and invite the siblings Barker rarely spoke about, she had expected it to be as simple as quick phone calls and instant confirmations. It had been easy to get their contact details from Barker's phone, but the rest of it had been anything but easy. Casper, the eldest brother, had been the only one to confirm that he would attend with his wife, Heather, during their first phone call. Ethan had called back after three days and agreed to come, but Theo had not picked up the phone at all, instead choosing to text Julia over a week later with a long list of questions, mainly revolving around the guest list. She had given up hopes of getting all of the Brown brothers together for Barker's thirty-ninth birthday, until Theo had sent a text message three days ago confirming his acceptance of her invitation.

"He's driving down tomorrow," Julia said. "He was the trickiest of you brothers to convince to come to this party."

Julia chuckled softly, hoping to make light of the difficult couple of weeks she had endured while organising everything, but her attempt at humour seemed to wash over their heads. Ethan rolled his eyes, as though he was not surprised, and Dawn looked uneasily at her husband.

"So, Bella *is* coming?" Luke asked, looking directly at Julia, his tone that of a boss demanding something from an employee. "Is she bringing Conrad?"

"I think so," Julia said, trying to remember exactly what Theo had said in his message. "He said there would be three of them. Him, his daughter, and her boyfriend. I'm assuming Conrad is the boyfriend?"

"No Michelle?" Dawn asked, almost under her breath at Ethan. "I guess the rumours *are* true."

"Michelle?" Julia asked. "I don't think I've heard that name."

"Theo's wife," Dawn said, arching a brow as though Julia should already know. "It's been obvious they've been heading for divorce ever since Bethany died. We hoped they'd patch it up, but people have been talking."

"Theo didn't mention anything about a wife," Julia confessed, not wanting to admit she also had no idea who Bethany was either. "Shall we set off? It might be a tight squeeze in my little car. I was only expecting the two of you."

"I'll walk," Jessie said, her fingers tapping rapidly on her phone screen. "I said I'd meet Dolly and

Dom anyway."

Before Julia could ask any questions, Jessie headed for the ticket office and out of the station without so much as a goodbye.

"She's going through a breakup," Julia explained quietly. "First boyfriend."

"Poor thing," Dawn said, looking at the exit of the station even though Jessie was already long gone. "Explains the clothes."

Julia's lips parted to let Dawn know that was how Jessie always dressed, but she decided against it, having spotted at least three visible designer logos on each of them.

With their bags in hand, they followed Julia out of the station to her aqua blue Ford Anglia, which was the only car in the middle of the empty car park.

"*Jesus Christ*," Luke muttered, his left brow arching high up his smooth forehead. "How *old* is that thing?"

"She's vintage," Julia said firmly, deciding she disliked Barker's nephew. "I promise she's fit for the road. She had a new engine fitted last month. I had a little accident in the middle of a storm."

"Same one that destroyed Barker's cottage?" Ethan asked as Julia unlocked the car boot. "I saw the pictures online. Where's he living now if his new cottage is wrecked?"

"With me," Julia said, taking Ethan's bag from him. "We're living together."

"Big step," Dawn said as she handed over her bag. "Must be serious?"

"I'd like to think so."

"I have *no* idea why Uncle Barker would want to live here," Luke said, his lip curling up as he looked around at the surrounding rolling fields. "It's the middle of nowhere."

"I quite like it," Dawn said, inhaling the crisp country air. "Makes a nice change from London."

"Thank God it's just for two days," Luke said as he thrust his bag into Julia's hand. "Be careful. My laptop is in there."

The three of them piled into Julia's car, Ethan taking the passenger seat. Julia crammed Luke's bag next to the other two, making sure to give it a nice heavy shove on the way.

Julia had wanted to meet Barker's family since the beginning of their relationship. All he had told her was that he had three brothers dotted around the country and that their mother had died five years ago. He had not mentioned names or ages, and every time Julia pushed the subject and asked when she would meet them, he would dismiss her with a vague '*soon*'. As Julia drove in the stuffy silence along the winding lane towards Peridale Manor, she wondered if there was a reason she knew very little about her partner's siblings.

"Your father lives *here?*" Dawn asked, clearly impressed when Peridale Manor came into view. "It's beautiful. Is that Cotswold stone?"

"It is," Julia said. "It's technically his father-in-law's house. It's been in the Wellington family for generations."

"Dawn is an architect," Ethan explained. "She does a lot of work for various London councils. She loves these big old buildings."

"They don't build them like this anymore," Dawn said, pulling out her phone to snap a picture through the window. "I'm glad I brought my sketch pad with me. I needed a break from glass and steel."

The gravel surrounding the house crunched under Julia's tyres when the lane ended. She pulled in between her father's black BMW and Katie's bright pink Range Rover.

"Looks like Casper is already here," Ethan said as he climbed out of the car, nodding at an orange Volkswagen Camper Van parked on the other side of the Range Rover. "I can't believe they're still in that old thing. He's been driving it for thirty years now."

After unloading their bags from the boot, they walked towards the double oak doors. Julia knocked hard on the wood, the door opening almost immediately. Hilary, the grumpy and, elderly housekeeper, peered through the gap, her eyeliner-circled eyes bulging out of her sockets like they always did.

"I thought there'd only be two of you," Hilary snapped, skipping the niceties as she looked down her nose at Julia. "You said there'd *only* be four guests arriving today. *Four*! I've only made up two bedrooms."

"That's my fault," Ethan said, holding his hands up. "I should have called ahead. I'm sure Luke won't mind sleeping on the couch. I'm Ethan, and this is my wife, Dawn."

Ethan held out his hand for Hilary, but she looked down at it as though he was offering her a slab of road kill they had found on the drive up. She huffed before swinging open the door and turning on her tiny heels.

"I've just polished the marble, so wipe your feet," she demanded as she shuffled to the grand sweeping staircase in the middle of the entrance hall. "I'll make up another room. Leave your bags near the door."

Julia wiped her feet on the doormat, smiling her apologies on behalf of Hilary. The housekeeper had been with the Wellington family for decades and was well past the age of retirement. Her loyalty to Vincent Wellington kept her there, even if the old man could no longer speak a word since his last stroke.

"This place is incredible," Dawn exclaimed, taking a picture of the glittering chandelier that hung from the ornate ceiling as she wiped her feet on the doormat. "Early 1800s?"

"I'm not sure," Julia replied. "Katie might know."

A man's deep laugh drifted out from the sitting room, echoing around the grand entrance hall. Dawn and Ethan looked at each other, both rolling their eyes.

"That'll be Casper," Ethan said with an exhausted sigh when he finished wiping his feet. "Always the bloody loudest in the room."

Julia was beginning to abandon all hope of a quiet family reunion for Barker's birthday.

Luke walked in and ignored the doormat, his eyes glued to his phone. He pushed the door shut with his hip, slamming it in its frame. Julia motioned for them to follow her towards the sitting room.

"*Julia*!" Brian, her father exclaimed, jumping up to kiss her on the cheek when she walked in. "You never told me Barker's brother was *the* Casper Brown!"

Julia smiled meekly at the couple sitting on the ornate red and gold couch across from her father. The man, who she assumed was Casper, looked to be the same age as Julia's father. He was plump, with a thick grey moustache balanced on his top lip. A cane sat between his legs, his hands leaning all of his weight onto it. The woman, Heather, was also plump, but was so short her feet did not touch the ground. Her thick grey hair had been set into neat rows, which Julia thought looked far too old-fashioned for her kind and open face, which was absent of any wrinkles thanks to her red chubby cheeks.

"Ethan," Casper said, nodding to his younger brother. "Dawn. Good to see you. How long's it been?"

"Bethany's funeral," Dawn reminded him.

"Ah, yes," Casper said, his eyes glazing over for a moment before turning to Julia with a wide grin. "You must be Julia! It's nice to put a face to the name."

"You never told us how pretty your daughter is, Brian," Heather said, looking around her husband to smile at Julia. "My brother-in-law has got himself a catch there."

"Do you all know each other?" Julia asked, glancing from her father to Casper.

"Casper was an avid collector of army medals," Brian explained. "We go back some twenty years. I'd say he bought more medals from me than any collector I've ever met."

"Still wasting your money on those things, Brother?" Ethan asked as he took in the large and lavishly decorated room. "I could think of better things to spend an army pension on, like a new car, for instance?"

"Your father is one of the best antique dealers there is," Casper said, looking at Julia and completely ignoring his brother's passive aggressive comment. "My hunt for medals became much harder when he got out of the business."

"I recently reacquired the antique barn," Brian said, clapping his hands together. "Anthony Kennedy croaked it, so I'm officially back in business. Murdered, in fact, and by his own mother, no less. I'd say I felt sorry for the fella, but he screwed over too many people on the way out. Got into some dodgy business with a fake Murphy Jones painting. Can't believe he was the best man at *both* of my weddings."

"Never did like him much," Casper muttered darkly. "He didn't know a medal from a chocolate coin. Still can't believe you're having another baby at your age, old boy. Our seven are all grown up now. Three boys, four girls. Our youngest, Daisy, has just gone off to university!"

"You're never too old," Brian said, rubbing his hands together and leaning forward. "And when you've got a wife as beautiful as mine, it's hard to resist."

"I'm thinking of trading this one in for a younger model," Casper joked, tapping Heather on the knee. "But I'm not sure if anyone will put up with an old codger like me with a fake leg."

He knocked on his left shin and an unnatural rattle of plastic shuddered under his trousers.

"The leg is the easiest part, Mr. Brown," Heather said, flicking her husband's ear. "I dare you to find someone else to put up with the *rest* of you."

Julia chuckled before looking at Dawn and Ethan, who could not have looked more disinterested with their relatives' banter. Julia had a feeling she was going to be getting along with Casper and Heather a lot more than anyone else during Barker's birthday party.

"I've got a nice collection of medals down at the barn," Brian said suddenly, clicking his fingers together. "I dare say even you don't have some of these. You'll have to come down and have a look tomorrow."

"Maybe," Casper said shakily, glancing unsurely at his wife. "My collection has – is that Luke?"

Casper squinted through Ethan and Dawn to his nephew, who was still glued to his phone. Luke looked up at his uncle Casper, a dry smile on his lips.

"Hello, Uncle," he said in such a cold way it made Julia shiver. "Auntie Heather. Nice to see you. How's things?"

Casper's eyes bulged out of his face, his jaw gritting, and his cheeks turning bright red in the process. For a split second, it seemed as though he was about to explode, but Heather softly rested her hand on his knee, rapidly sedating him. Julia scanned the faces of the others in the room, but no one else seemed to notice the obvious tension.

"*Lemonade!*" a squeaky voice announced as metal wheels rattled along the polished floorboards. "Oh, more guests! I'll have to grab some more glasses."

Julia turned to see her father's wife, Katie Wellington-South, pushing in a trolley with a large jug of Wellington family lemonade and four glasses. Her peroxide blonde hair was curled to perfection, her face painted like a model, and her ample chest and giant stomach looked fit to bursting out of her tight shirt.

"None for me," Casper said, pushing himself up on his cane with a groan. "I-I-It's been a long day, and I think I need to lie down. My good leg is cramping up."

"Are we okay to go up?" Heather asked, standing up and resting her hand on her husband's lower back. "It's better that he rests up now before it gets any worse. He's not used to wearing the prosthetic for this long. I told him to take it off while I was driving, but he never listens. Was more worried about having it on in case we crashed, but at the speed I was driving, I think a plastic leg would have been the least of his worries."

"You're in the room at the end of the hall near the bust of my great-grandfather," Katie announced after pushing the trolley around to the other side of the couch. "You can't miss it."

Katie rested her hands on the bottom of her

lower back and pushed out her stomach. Julia looked down at her high heels, almost not believing that she still insisted on wearing them so close to the end of her pregnancy.

Casper and Heather hobbled past them, their smiles warm and kind until they landed on Luke. For a split second, the pressure boiled up again, turning the room cold until they left. Julia itched to know what was causing the tension, but was too polite to ask either of them.

"I think I could use a nap too," Dawn said, pinching between her eyes. "I can feel one of my migraines brewing."

"I'll come up with you," Ethan said, opening his mouth and letting out what seemed to be a fake yawn. "That train journey has exhausted me."

"You're in the room next door to your brother," Katie announced, pouring homemade lemonade into two glasses. "Are you staying for a glass, Julia?"

"I should get back," Julia said, hooking her thumb over her shoulder, not wanting to admit that the lemonade was too sickly for her tastes. "Barker will be wondering where I am."

"What's the Wi-Fi password?" Luke asked bluntly, the last of Barker's family still in the room. "I need to check my emails."

As Katie shuffled over to the internet router on a small table in the corner of the room, Julia nodded for her father to follow her out into the hall.

"Is everything sorted?" Julia asked, pulling a small notepad out of her coat pocket to run down her list again. "Did the balloons arrive?"

"*Everything* is in hand," he assured her with a confident smile that she knew was supposed to soothe her, but did not. "I've told you not to worry. Just bake one of your delicious cakes, and everything will go smoothly."

"I never expected it to be so difficult," she said, slotting the notepad back into her pocket. "I never expected *them* to be so difficult. I'm beginning to wonder if this was all a giant mistake. What was that look Casper gave Luke?"

"What look? You have nothing to worry about with Casper and Heather," he assured her as they walked to the front door, their heels clicking on the shiny marble. "They're the loveliest people I know. This world just keeps getting smaller, doesn't it? I've known Barker all this time, and I never put the two Browns together."

"The last brother, Theo, is arriving tomorrow at noon. Do you want me to be here to greet them?"

"It's *all* taken care of," he repeated, yanking on

the door. "There's nothing to panic about. The Wellington family are famous for their hospitality. We'll have a nice dinner tonight. They'll be refreshed for tomorrow night's party, you'll see."

"Okay," she said, allowing herself to smile for a second, glad she only had the cake to worry about now. "Just don't let them anywhere near the village. The last thing I want is for Barker to see one of them so close to the party."

"I'll keep them under lock and key," he promised with a wink. "Go home, put your feet up, and have one of those peppermint teas you like. What could go wrong?"

Leaving her father on the doorstep, Julia climbed back into her car at the exact moment it began to rain. Reversing out of the tight space, she waved to her father before turning and heading back down the winding lane. As her window wipers squeaked against the glass, she inhaled deeply, wondering why she felt even more nervous than she had standing on the platform waiting to meet one of Barker's brothers for the first time.

"What could go wrong?" she whispered to herself, repeating her father's words. "What could *possibly* go wrong?"

CHAPTER 2

Julia awoke the exact moment her phone began to vibrate the next morning. She immediately stopped the alarm, holding her breath as she looked down at Barker in the dark. He snorted, rolled over, and resumed snoring into his pillow. He would be fast asleep until his alarm woke him.

Julia tossed back the covers and climbed carefully out of bed, the cold floorboards creaking underfoot. She could not remember the last time she had woken up before the radiators came on. Glad she had left her sheepskin slippers next to her bed the previous night, she slipped her feet into them as she stood up. Avoiding the notoriously squeaky floorboards, she tiptoed across the room, grabbing her pink dressing gown from the hook on the side of her wardrobe.

"Morning, boy," she whispered to Mowgli, her grey Maine Coon, as he crawled out from his warm spot underneath the bed. "Bit early for you, isn't it?"

Mowgli shook out his flattened fur, his sleepy eyes still half-closed. He nudged her leg with the side of his soft face, letting her know it was never too early for breakfast.

With Mowgli dancing around her ankles, Julia crept out of the bedroom, glancing at Barker one last time.

"Happy Birthday," she whispered.

Once in the kitchen, Julia flicked on the spotlights under the cupboards, not wanting to turn on the ceiling lights in case the bright light disturbed the rest of the household. Letting out a long yawn, she filled the kettle from the tap. She looked out into her slightly overgrown back garden, the sky still inky, the grass still frosty.

While the kettle boiled, Julia plopped a peppermint and liquorice teabag into her favourite giant mug, fed Mowgli, and began gathering the basic ingredients for Barker's birthday cake. He likely knew that she was going to bake him a cake, but she thought the sheer size of the one she intended to bake might give away her plans for more people than the quiet dinner he expected.

She stepped back and looked at the self-raising flour, butter, eggs, caster sugar, and baking powder. She decided against pulling out the various flavourings and colourings until she needed them. The fewer ingredients pointing to a birthday cake, the easier it would be to pretend she was baking something for the café if Barker suddenly woke up. The soft snoring coming from the slightly ajar bedroom door let her know that was not likely to happen anytime soon.

With the oven preheating, Julia began measuring out enough sponge cake ingredients to fill eight sandwich tins. She planned to colour each layer differently, but her practice runs had taught her it would be easier to change the colours when she had separated the mixture into each tin.

Barker probably expected Julia to make him one of her famous double fudge chocolate cakes. It was his favourite, after all, but she had been making that same cake on an almost weekly basis since the beginning of their relationship. Since it was his birthday, she had been planning something a little more special, but no less delicious.

One of the few things Julia knew about Barker's mother, aside from that she also loved baking and apparently cursed like a sailor, was that her favourite cake was coconut cakes. Julia loved coconut too, so when she had come up with the idea to gather Barker's brothers, she had decided a variation of a coconut cake would be an easy crowd pleaser. After seeing how strained Casper and Ethan's relationship seemed to have been yesterday, and how dismissively Ethan had spoken about Theo, Julia hoped their late mother's favourite cake would somehow bring them together. She knew it was a long shot, but her baking had performed seemingly impossible miracles before.

When she was happy with the consistency of the batter, she sprinkled in a healthy dose of desiccated coconut along with two caps of pure coconut extract before dividing it between the eight tins. When she was satisfied she had poured them evenly by eye, something her mother had taught her to do as a child rather than relying on scales for every step,

Julia gathered the colourings from the cupboard and started mixing. She watched as the beige batter turned purple, blue, green, yellow, orange, pink, turquoise, and red, the bright colours bringing a little sunshine to the dark and chilly morning. After adding extra racks to the oven, she carefully placed the raw mixtures into the heat, set her timer to twenty-five minutes, and finally grabbed her peppermint and liquorice tea. Despite it being free of caffeine, nothing woke her up more than the minty sweetness of her favourite hot drink.

Remembering the pizza boxes in the sitting room from the takeaway the night before, Julia hugged her tea as she wandered through. She was surprised to see Jessie wrapped up in a blanket on the couch, and even more surprised that she was wide awake, staring at the television while Julia's *Pretty Woman* DVD played almost silently in the dark.

"*Jessie?*" Julia whispered, not wanting to startle her. "Are you alright? What are you doing up?"

"I couldn't sleep," she whispered back, wiping her cold red nose with the edge of the blanket. "You always watch *Pretty Woman* to cheer you up, so I thought it was worth a shot."

"Is it working?"

"I still want to punch Julia Roberts every time she cackles at that jewellery box," Jessie said, sitting up, the blanket wrapped around her head and shoulders. "I'd say it was half successful."

Julia handed over her tea, which Jessie accepted gratefully. She sipped the warm drink, her eyes blank as they stared at the burnt logs in the whistling fireplace.

"Is there something wrong with me?" Jessie asked, frowning into her tea. "Every time something is going well, it seems to go wrong."

"Oh, Jessie," Julia said, wrapping her arm tightly around her shoulders. "It's not your fault. Things like this – they just happen. You'll meet other boys, and you'll fall in love again."

"I don't want to," she said after another sip of the tea. "They're a waste of space. Billy sent me a text last night asking me not to end things."

"What did you say?"

"I told him I wasn't being an army wife who waits for their boyfriend to get back or not get back from wars," Jessie said. "It's stupid. He's only joining up because he thinks he'll never get a job in Peridale. I bet it's his dad who put the idea in his head. He never once spoke about it, and then all of a sudden it's a dream he's always had but just forgot to tell me. How does that make any sense?"

"Men are complicated," Julia said, squeezing her shoulder reassuringly. "Simple, and yet incredibly complicated creatures."

"They're *idiots*," Jessie said, her brows drawing together in a frown. "What's the point?"

Julia was not sure she could answer. She had a failed twelve-year marriage under her belt and was only into her first year with Barker. She loved him with all of her heart and was glad she had met him when she did because she was old enough to appreciate their relationship. How could she explain that to a seventeen-year-old girl?

"One day you'll meet someone who'll make you understand why it's worth it," Julia assured her, watching as Mowgli padded into the room licking his lips. "Until then, live your life for you."

Jessie exhaled heavily and finished the last of the tea, which was uncharacteristic for her. She rested the empty cup in her lap and stared at the leafy dregs in the bottom as though reading her own fortune. When she did not see what she wanted, she cast the cup onto the stack of pizza boxes on the floor and melted into Julia's side.

"Get some sleep," Julia whispered as she stroked the back of her hair through the fluffy blanket.

"Mondays are always quiet. Come into the café when you're ready, or not at all. I'll manage on my own for one day."

Jessie rubbed her tired eyes and nodded. With the blanket still wrapped around her shoulders, she walked back to her bedroom.

There were times when Jessie caught Julia off guard by how grown-up she seemed, and other times she looked like a lost little girl; this morning was an example of the latter.

Something vibrated and lit up where Jessie had been sitting. It was her mobile phone, and a text message had just come through from Billy. Julia did not realise she was reading a preview of the message until it was too late. '*I love you. Please text me, we need to-*'. Leaving the phone where Jessie had left it, Julia turned off the television and walked back into the kitchen to start work on the coconut buttercream to spread in between the rainbow slices.

"It's all part of growing up," Julia assured Mowgli as he begged for attention on the corner of the counter. "She'll be okay."

***

BARKER'S ALARM WENT OFF A LITTLE after sunrise, but Julia was already waiting by the bed with a full English breakfast, a rack of toast, and a cup of coffee.

"Good morning," she smiled before kissing him gently on the forehead. "Happy Birthday, Barker."

"Breakfast in bed?" he asked, his voice faint and croaky. "I wish it was my birthday every day."

Barker sat up in bed, letting the covers fall into his lap. Julia placed one of her pillows on his knees and balanced the tray carefully on top, the bacon and sausages still piping hot.

"How long have you been up?" Barker asked, rubbing his eyes as he stared down at the food. "It's early."

"Not long," she lied. "About half an hour."

Julia failed to mention she had finished constructing his birthday cake, successfully hidden it at the back of the fridge, baked a decoy chocolate cake along with two-dozen cupcakes for the café, wrapped his birthday present, showered, and eaten her own breakfast.

She perched on the edge of their bed, and watched him wolf down his breakfast. Before officially moving in, Barker had been splitting his time between his cottage down the lane and hers, but since having him there full time, she had come to appreciate how much of a good mood it put her in waking up next to him every single morning. In the short time they had been living together, they had painted over the magnolia walls in the bedroom with a soft shade of dusky blue, bought a brand new king size wooden bed complete with new bedding, matching bedside tables, and a new wardrobe for Barker's work shirts. Julia could barely remember the time it had just been her bedroom.

"Is Jessie up yet?" Barker asked through a mouthful of toast, crumbs and melted butter on his stubbly chin.

"I told her to sleep in," Julia said, not wanting to mention their early morning chat. "I think she's struggling with this whole Billy situation."

Barker sighed as he moved the beans around his plate with his fork. He looked up at Julia, a hesitant smile on his face.

"I care about Jessie, but –"

"You can't help but think it's for the best?"

"I'm not alone then," Barker said, a little more confidently. "The amount of trouble that boy got into when I first moved to this village. There wasn't a week that went by when I didn't arrest him for something. I know he was starting to change, and underneath it all, he's actually a sweet kid, but the army might be just what he needs. Structure and discipline are underrated these days. It'll make him grow up."

"He told her he loves her," Julia whispered, not wanting to risk Jessie overhearing despite knowing she was probably in a deep sleep by now. "I think she loves him too."

"Do you remember being seventeen and thinking that you were in love for real?" Barker asked, dropping his fork onto the plate. "Mine was Stacey Crenshaw. I think they go by Simon Crenshaw these days, but that's not the point. She'll meet other guys."

"Sue and Neil met when they were seventeen," Julia said, thinking about her sister's happy relationship. "They're both thirty-two, married, and she's pregnant with his twins."

"Do you really see that for Jessie?"

"I don't know," Julia admitted, unsure of what she saw for the teen. "I take things one day at a time. She's more fragile than she comes across."

"And tougher than you give her credit for." Barker placed the tray on the edge of his bedside table and jumped out of bed in his black boxer briefs. He picked up his dressing gown, which he always left on the floor next to the bed, and pulled it on. "That girl has been through a lot this year. Good and bad. It wasn't that long ago that she was stabbed in that attic after being kidnapped by that mad woman. Most fully-grown adults would crumble to bits after something like that, and she's still going."

"I know she's strong," Julia said. "I know that better than anyone. I just want her to be happy, but that's not realistic, is it? Life is messy and complex."

"And she needs to go through it," Barker said as he kissed Julia on the top of the head. "You've given that girl a life she was never going to have, but you can't protect her from everything."

Julia sighed, but she reluctantly nodded. She knew Barker was completely right. She could try her best to be there for Jessie through everything, but she would never become the woman she was destined to be if she did not face all the real world had to offer. She had seen more than most going through the social care system and living on the streets, but there was still so much for her to figure out.

"Thanks for breakfast. It was delicious."

"Breakfast in bed isn't the end of it," Julia said, eager to push her mind back onto Barker's birthday. "Your present is in the dining room."

Julia nodded her permission for him to go and look. She followed him into the dining room, where the giant rectangular box waited for him.

"I used two whole rolls," Julia said, standing in the doorway with her arms crossed. "It was harder to wrap than it looks."

Barker tore off the corner and pulled off a large strip of the paper, the colourful picture of the television jumping out on the front of the box.

"A new TV?" Barker cried, the grin continuing to grow. "Sixty-two inches?"

"And it's 4K and 3D and all those other nonsense words you said you wanted," Julia said, pulling off the rest of the paper. "I don't understand what's wrong with the one I have, but you seemed to really want a new one, so I thought I'd sacrifice half of the sitting room for the sake of this mammoth screen."

"You have no idea how much I love you right now," Barker said, wrapping his arms around her neck. "We can put the old one in the bedroom so we can watch movies in bed."

"That decision will need some more discussion," Julia said. "I was thinking of offering it to Jessie so she could watch what she wanted in private. I might order her one of those stick things so she can watch things off the internet."

"'*One of those stick things*'?" Barker asked playfully. "You sound like your gran right now. Next, you're going to tell me you miss the days of VHS and mobile phones with buttons."

"The buttons *were* easier to use," she said with a shrug. "You should get ready for work. You can play with your new toy when you get home."

Barker kissed her softly before slipping into the bathroom. When steam drifted from under the door, Julia carefully opened Jessie's door, popping her head around the edge. Jessie was curled up on top of her bed, a pillow clutched to her chest as she snored softly.

"Sleep tight," Julia whispered before closing the door again.

Julia quickly dressed for work, opting for blue jeans and a navy blouse; it was far too cold to have exposed legs today. She waited by the front door in her pink pea coat while Barker ironed his suit in the hallway in nothing more than his underwear. When he was finally dressed, he grabbed his briefcase, and they drove into the village together in Julia's car.

"I'll see you at lunch," Barker said, kissing her on the cheek as he opened the door. "I expect a huge slice of chocolate cake today of all days."

"Consider it done."

They parted ways, leaving Julia to open the café. She was thankful that Mondays were always quiet because it allowed her to perform her weekly stock check and to deep clean the place. The bell above the door did not ring out until nearly noon.

"Excuse me," a young and fashionably dressed woman said, one hand still on the door. "We're looking for directions to Peridale Manor. Do you have any idea where that is?"

Julia stepped around the counter, a crease in her brow. She dusted her flour-covered hands down her apron, glancing out of the window at the car the girl had exited. Julia could almost not believe who was behind the wheel.

"*Ethan?*" Julia mumbled, squinting through the window. "Why is Ethan in the village?"

"Huh?" the girl asked, whipping her brown and blonde ombré curls over her shoulder. "What do you mean?"

"The man driving that car," Julia said, extending a finger to the slender, bald man behind the wheel. "I told my dad to keep him at Peridale Manor."

The girl looked at the man Julia was pointing at. She seemed just as confused as Julia felt for a moment, before tossing her head back to let out a high-pitched laugh.

"Is your name Julia?" the girl asked, clicking her fingers together. "That would make *total* sense."

"I am," Julia said with a nod. "Who are you?"

"Bella," she said. "Bella Brown. That's not Ethan, that's my father, Theo. They're twins."

"Oh," Julia said, feeling her cheeks turning bright red. "I should have really known that, shouldn't I?"

"It's okay," Bella said with a shrug, pulling her phone out of her pocket. "It used to happen all the time before – well, when they were closer. Haven't seen Uncle Ethan since the funeral. So, you're Uncle Barker's girlfriend?"

Julia nodded and watched as Bella pouted into the camera of her phone, taking a selfie against Julia's pink and blue wallpaper. She changed facial expressions half a dozen times, snapping away like she was in the middle of a photo-shoot.

"The lighting in here is *too* perfect," Bella exclaimed, looking around the small café. "Maybe I should get Conrad in here for a couple's selfie?"

Julia looked into the car, where a tanned, handsome young man with bright blond hair was sitting in the passenger seat. Theo, who looked eerily like his brother, but without the crooked nose, bobbed his head to see what was taking his daughter so long.

"I've never really been one for selfies," Julia confessed, almost apologetically. "We had film cameras when I was your age, and it wasn't as fun when you had to wait for them to develop."

"It's for my followers," Bella said as she adjusted the lighting and colours on the picture she had just taken, transforming it into something that looked almost professional. "I have eleven thousand. Conrad's almost at one hundred. It's easier to get followers when you have abs these days, don't you think?"

"One hundred?" Julia laughed awkwardly. "I think I have thirty-four Facebook friends. I don't think I know one hundred people."

"Oh, I meant one hundred *thousand*," Bella said with a shrug as though the number meant nothing. "I don't know how he deals with the pressure, but I guess it's his job now."

"He makes money from selfies?"

"Companies pay him to advertise their stuff," Bella said, glancing back at her boyfriend in the car, who was engrossed with whatever was happening on his phone. "Teeth whitening products, food supplements, detox teas, clothes, you name it. *Hey*! I could probably get him to give you a discount to shout-out your café! I suppose we're family now, aren't we?"

"I suppose we are," Julia said with an anxious smile, understanding virtually none of what the girl was talking about. "I'll have to think about that."

"Directions?" the girl asked after Theo honked on the horn three times in quick succession. "It's been a long drive."

"Right," Julia said, turning and grabbing her notepad from the counter to scribble down a crude map. "If you go up past The Plough, take a right at the B&B, and continue onto Mulberry Lane, you'll pass an antique barn. Take a right, and then a left, and you'll see a sign at the bottom of a winding lane that will point you in the right direction. That's the quickest way from here. You can't miss it."

"Thank you," Bella said, looking down at the map with a tilted head. "I suppose I'll see you later at the party."

"I suppose you will," Julia said, pushing forward a polite smile. "It was lovely to meet you, Bella."

"You too, Julie."

"It's Juli-*a*."

"Right," she said, pointing at Julia as she walked backwards out of the café, the map clenched against her phone. "I'll remember that. See-ya!"

The young woman spun around, her stylish hair bouncing over her shoulder. She jumped into the car and passed the map to her father. She said something that made Theo bob down and stare through the window at Julia. Julia waved and smiled, but the man did not bother to return it. He sped off, the tyres screeching as he went.

"Oh, Julia," she whispered to herself as she spotted Jessie wandering down the lane from their cottage. "What have you got yourself into?"

CHAPTER 3

"Dot," Barker said through a strained smile. "You shouldn't have."

"Oh, it was no bother!" Dot waved her hand dismissively as she leaned back in her chair with a pleased smile. "I saw it and *immediately* thought of you."

"'*How To Survive Your Midlife Crisis*'," Sue, Julia's sister, read the title aloud over his shoulder.

"Can I borrow that for my Neil when you're finished?"

"I'm only thirty-nine," Barker said, his cheeks flushing as he placed the book on the table next to his half-finished slice of chocolate cake. "It's the thought that counts I suppose."

"You're displaying *all* the classic symptoms," Dot announced with another wave of her hand. "*Anyone* can see it."

"The symptoms?" Julia asked, sending a playful wink across the dining table to Barker as she sucked the chocolate off her fork. "Please, do enlighten us, Gran."

"Well, that *ridiculous* television speaks for itself," Dot cried, craning her neck to look at the new set in the sitting room. "It's like a *cinema*! What's wrong with a nice little eleven-inch screen?"

"It was a gift!" Barker cried defensively, looking at Julia for support. "Julia bought it. If anyone is having the crisis, it's her."

"You *did* ask for it," she replied with a shrug. "*Classic* symptom, like Gran says."

"They used to make TVs that small?" Jessie mumbled, looking up from her plate as she traced her fork around the outline of her untouched chocolate cake. "Sounds pointless."

"What are the other symptoms, Gran?" Sue asked, smirking at Julia as she rubbed her firm bump. "Keep going."

"*Weight gain!*" Dot cried, poking Barker's soft stomach. "I've said it before, and I'll say it again, all of those cakes aren't doing you any good, Barker Brown!"

"It's my birthday!" he mumbled through a mouthful of chocolate icing. "I'm exactly the same weight I was this time last year."

"And this idea that you're going to write a crime book?" Dot exclaimed, casting a finger over to the vintage typewriter in the corner. "*Classic* symptom. Stick to what you know, and that's being an average detective inspector!"

Sue choked on her glass of water as she stared ahead at Julia with the usual look of '*did Gran really just say that?*' plastered across her face.

"Classic," Julia echoed.

"It would do you some good to have a read. I flicked through, and I found it *very* informative."

Dot stamped her finger down on the book, but Barker could not have looked any less interested if he had tried. He stabbed his fork into the cake, stuffing even more into his mouth. Julia and Sue could barely contain their laughter.

"Mine next," Sue said, reaching across the table, her large bump getting in the way. "It's not as *helpful* as Gran's, but I think you'll like it."

Sue slid the glittery pink-wrapped box down the table. Barker ripped back the paper, seeming a little more relieved than he had looked when opening Dot's.

"My favourite aftershave," Barker said with a genuine smile. "Thank you, Sue. I can actually *use* this. I was running low."

"I know," Sue replied with a confident nod. "I was poking around your bathroom last week. I didn't know what to get you, and then it came to me like an epiphany when I was sitting on the toilet. All men like aftershave!"

"Men smelt like *men* back in my day," Dot exclaimed, grabbing the box from Barker to read over the label. "'*A spicy, aromatic scent with hints of vanilla*'. Sounds like a curry, and you know my stomach doesn't do well with foreign food."

Jessie giggled from under her hood at the end of the table. It caught everyone off guard, including Jessie, who seemed to have briefly forgotten about her break-up.

"Well, if you'll excuse me, nature calls," Barker said, pushing his chair away from the table with a defeated look. "Don't tell me, Dot. Is that another symptom?"

"Actually, I *think* it is," Dot said, picking up the book to flick through the mass of pages. "I'm *sure* I read something about it in here."

Barker laughed with a shake of his head, brushing his hand across Julia's back as he walked out of the room. None of them moved until they heard the lock on the bathroom door click into place.

"Do you think he knows?" Sue whispered excitedly, bolting up in her chair. "Does he think this is his real party?"

"Of course he doesn't know," Dot cried, tossing the book onto the table. "He's a man! He hasn't figured out a thing. He probably thinks this is his real present."

"It *isn't?*" Julia asked, turning the book over in her hand. "I thought you were being serious."

"Picked it up for twenty pence in the charity shop," Dot said with a thin grin, adjusting the brooch holding her stiff white collar in place. "I have a card in my bag with a gift voucher for his favourite clothes shop."

"He has a favourite clothes shop?" Jessie asked, scrunching up her nose. "All his shirts look the same."

"That's because he buys them all from the *same* shop," Dot exclaimed, tapping the side of her nose. "I let myself in when you were all at work. Had a nice look through his wardrobe."

"I need to change the locks," Julia said, her eyes wide as she gathered up the plates. "Did you put the real birthday cake in the boot of my car, Sue?"

"Done," Sue said, pushing herself up from the seat. "What time is Katie calling?"

"In about ten minutes," Julia said after checking the grandfather clock in the corner of the room. "Hopefully they've got everything sorted up there. You should all start leaving when he gets out of the bathroom."

"I need to pee before I go," Sue said as she shuffled to the door, her giant stomach poking out through her fluttering shirt. "The twins have been kicking my bladder all day. I'm sure one of them is trying out for the Premier League."

Julia dumped the dishes in the kitchen sink while Sue waited by the bathroom door clutching her lower back. When the toilet flushed and Barker unlocked the door, Sue barged in, quickly locking it behind her.

"*Must dash!*" Dot exclaimed, hurrying out of the

dining room with her handbag slung over her shoulder. "Enjoy your book, Barker. Some of the girls and I have joined a film club, and we're starting our *Saw* marathon tonight. According to Amy Clark, the films are about jigsaws or something. I wasn't really paying much attention, but I like a jigsaw as much as the next person."

Dot kissed Julia on the cheek and slapped Barker heartily on the shoulder before heading out of the front door, the cold wind blowing down the hallway behind her.

"That woman is something else," Barker said with a disbelieving shake of his head as he stared at the door. "*Midlife crisis?*"

"I'm going to Dolly and Dom's," Jessie said, her hood low over her eyes as she hurried for the door. "Bye."

The door slammed behind her, letting more cold air into the hallway. Sue hobbled out of the bathroom, wiping her damp hands on the back of her stretchy maternity trousers.

"Neil will be expecting me back," Sue said, rubbing her belly rhythmically. "He's insisting on reading the bump bedtime stories. Can you believe they're as big as pineapples now? I'm sure they're just as prickly too. Pregnancy is more uncomfortable than anyone ever tells you."

Sue kissed them both on the cheek, grabbed her handbag from the dining room, and waddled out of the cottage.

"And then there were two," Barker said, looking around the empty cottage. "Not how I was expecting to spend my birthday."

"You said you wanted a quiet one," Julia reminded him as she filled the sink with hot water. "Places to be, and all that."

"Dot and Sue were only here for twenty minutes," Barker said, scratching the side of his head as he consulted his watch. "Oh, well. At least there's more cake left."

"Actually, I was hoping to sell the rest of it in the café tomorrow," Julia said as she squirted washing up liquid into the sink. "Sorry!"

"Right," he said, sighing as he slapped his hands against his sides. "Well, I suppose I'll go and watch the six o'clock news in 3D then."

Barker planted himself on the couch with another long sigh. Julia smirked to herself as she quickly washed the plates. She felt bad for still lying to him, but these were the last lies she would have to tell. She could not wait for the party to be over so she could go back to being honest Julia.

"It'll be worth it," she whispered to herself as she rinsed the last plate before placing it on the metal draining board. "I hope."

Right on cue, the phone on the kitchen wall rattled in its frame. Julia let it ring for a moment, not answering until she was satisfied Barker had heard.

"Hello?" she said, already knowing who was on the other end.

"*Julia?*" Katie's shaky voice crackled down the phone. "Julia, something terrible has happened."

"*What's happened?*" Julia called loud enough so that Barker could hear. "You want us to come to Peridale Manor immediately?"

"No, Julia, I'm being serious," Katie said, the sudden depth of her usually squeaky voice knotting fear inside of Julia. "It's Luke, Barker's nephew. He's – *He's dead.*"

CHAPTER 4

"I – I don't understand," Barker muttered as they sped up the winding lane towards Peridale Manor in the dark, the headlights illuminating the bushes fencing them in. "Why is my nephew at your dad's house? It doesn't make any sense."

"It's all my fault," Julia said, pushing her curls from her eyes as she sped around the tight corner.

"I've been planning a surprise birthday party for you. I invited everyone. Katie was supposed to call to let me know they were ready, and I was going to get us up to the manor."

"Who are '*they*'?"

"Your three brothers," Julia said. "Heather and Dawn too, and Bella and her boyfriend, and – and *Luke*."

"I don't understand," he repeated.

"I borrowed your phone," she confessed as she rigidly held back her tears, her foot pushing down on the accelerator. "I called them all. My dad said he would host them for the party."

"No, I meant I don't understand how you got them *all* to agree to come here," Barker said, his fingers rubbing the temples on the sides of his head. "After Bethany's funeral, I didn't think they would ever agree to being in the same room again."

"I'm sorry," Julia apologised, tears streaming down her face, aware of how fast she was driving, but unable to lift her foot. "Oh, Barker. I shouldn't have meddled."

"Julia, slow down."

"Your nephew is dead, and it's all my fault."

"*Julia!*"

Barker's hands slapped down on the dashboard,

forcing Julia to slam her foot on the brakes. The tyres screeched along the gravel, halting right behind three shadowy figures in front of the manor. They turned around, their confused faces illuminated by the flashing lights of the three police cars parked in front of them.

"*Julia?*" Dot cried, squinting through the front window of the car, Jessie and Sue next to her. "What on Earth -"

Julia rubbed the tears from her lashes, inhaling deeply, the guilt too much to bear. Barker squeezed her knee firmly, but it did not reassure her.

"You almost *hit* us!" Dot cried. "What are you *playing* at?"

"Well, she didn't hit you," Barker said, jumping out of the car and walking straight past them towards the officers guarding the front door. "I need to find out what's going on."

Julia peeled her fingers off the steering wheel and got out of the car, her legs like jelly. She took a deep breath as her trembling fingers tucked her curls behind her ears.

"How did this happen?" Julia asked, gulping down her added guilt for almost hitting her family. "I don't understand."

"Well, you almost bloody turned us into

pancakes!" Dot cried. "That's what happened."

"She means the *murder*," Jessie mumbled from under her hood, less bothered about almost being hit by Julia's car.

"*Murder?*" Julia echoed. "How?"

"Strangled, according to one of the officers," Sue said, wrapping her arms around her body as the bitter wind picked up around them. "We've only just arrived ourselves. They won't let us in."

"*Strangled?*" Julia whispered, looking past her family to the yellowy light flooding out of the manor's front doors. "Where's Dad?"

"You've got *no chance* of getting inside," Dot said, wafting her hands as she stared at the officers talking to Barker by the front door. "I told them I was family, but they won't let me in, and they won't let anyone out!"

"We could always try the back door," Jessie suggested with a shrug, hooking her thumb to the dark side of the house. "That's always an option."

"Hey, we *could* try the back door!" Dot echoed as though it had been her idea. "That's a great idea."

"*My* great idea."

"The details don't matter," Dot said as she linked her arm through Sue's. "Are you okay to walk?"

"I'm pregnant, not an invalid," Sue said, following it up by immediately by wincing. "Although I am carrying twins, aren't I? Maybe I'll wait in the car."

"I think you should all stay here," Julia said, her nerves dying down long enough for her brain to engage. "If the police aren't letting people inside, it's because the house is a crime scene, and three new people walking around are going to be easier to spot than one."

"You're not invisible, Julia," Dot exclaimed through pursed lips, clearly upset that Julia was putting a stop to her snooping. "You're wearing a bright pink coat, for Christ's sake!"

Julia shrugged off the heavy coat, the November chill consuming her in seconds. She tossed it to her gran, who reluctantly joined Sue in the car.

"Be careful," Jessie said, smiling softly at Julia. "Don't do anything I wouldn't."

"I'm just going to find out what's happened," she said, running her thumb along Jessie's soft, cold cheek. "I feel responsible for this."

Julia crept to the edge of the gravel driveway, avoiding the blue flashing lights. Her dark jeans and navy blouse faded in nicely with the forest that enclosed the vast grounds around the manor.

Julia stuck to the side of the house, ducking down past the tall windows. She reached a door, which she knew opened into one of Hilary's cleaning supply cupboards. She rattled the handle, but it was locked. Julia pressed on, creeping to the back of the grand house. As she transferred from the damp grass onto the stone patio, light flooded out from the kitchen through the double French doors. Holding her breath, Julia crept up to the kitchen window and peered inside to make sure the coast was clear; it was not.

The girl she had met earlier in her café, Bella, was sitting at the kitchen island, sobbing into her hands, with her handsome blond boyfriend, Conrad, comforting her with a blank stare. Julia slid across the wall and rattled the doors, but they were also locked.

"*Hello?*" she called softly with a gentle knock on the glass. "Can you let me in?"

The young couple practically jumped out of their skins before whipping around to face Julia. They squinted into the dark garden, a glimmer of recognition on the young woman's mascara-streaked face.

"Conrad, that's Barker's girlfriend," she stammered, sliding off the stool, her mobile phone clutched in her hand. "Julie."

"It's Juli-*a*," she reminded the girl with a frustrated smile. "Can you let me in? It's cold out here."

Bella and Conrad looked at each other as though considering whether they should ignore Julia like a stray cat.

"They told us not to leave," Bella called, taking a small step forward. "The murderer might be out there."

"I'm not the murderer," Julia said with a disbelieving laugh. "I've only just arrived with Barker."

Bella chewed the inside of her lip, looking at Conrad for permission. The attractive young man could only offer a meek shrug.

Julia rubbed her hands together in front of her face and blew her hot breath into her cupped palms. It had the desired effect. Bella rushed to unlock the door, opening it just enough for Julia to slip inside before locking it again.

"Thank you," she said through chattering teeth. "It's not much warmer in here, is it?"

Bella shook her head as she retreated to Conrad's side. He wrapped his arm around her again, his eyes trained on the tiled floor. He looked like he had been crying too, pale streaks running down his bronze face, letting her know his tan likely came from a bottle rather than the sun.

"Do you know what happened?" Julia asked eagerly as she warmed up. "I heard he was strangled."

Bella tossed her head back and let out a shrill wail. She pushed her face into Conrad's white shirt, which was already stained with her mascara tears.

"It's like Bethany all over again," she sobbed, her voice muffled in her boyfriend's toned pectorals. "I can't deal with this again."

"It'll be okay," Conrad said, his voice softer and fainter than Julia would have expected from someone with such a strong jaw and solid nose. "You'll get through this. You're a fighter, and you have your Bella Belles."

"Bella Belles?" Julia asked, looking around the empty kitchen. "Is that a flower?"

"It's what I call my followers," Bella said, sniffling and pulling away from Conrad's shirt. "They're never going to believe this. Maybe I should live stream now and let them all know what's happened?"

"It might boost your follower count," Conrad said with a supportive shrug. "Channel your pain, baby."

"It's probably best that you *don't*," Julia said, feeling like she was talking to freshly landed aliens from a distant world. "The police will want to talk to you, and it might cause you some trouble if you put your story out there before you tell them."

"*Police?*" Conrad cried, his bottom lip trembling. "We – *We* didn't do anything. *We* didn't *kill* him."

"Why *would* we?" Bella cried, her pretty face twisting tightly. "He was my *cousin*."

"It's just procedure," Barker said as he walked into the kitchen. "Julia. Why am I not surprised to see you've somehow found your way in here?"

"*Uncle Barker!*" Bella cried before running into his arms like a little girl. "Oh, what an awful thing to happen on your birthday."

"Forget my birthday," he said as he rubbed her hair where the brown faded into blonde. "It's good to see you, kiddo."

"It's just like Bethany all over again," she repeated, her sobs somehow more genuine now that she was with her uncle and not thinking about her '*Bella Belles*'. "Why our family?"

"Bethany's death was an accident," he said, pulling her away and holding her shoulders. "This was not. Someone murdered Luke."

"Who?" Conrad asked, his hand drifting up to his mouth as though the confirmation from Barker somehow made it real. "Who would want to do such a thing?"

"I – *I* don't know," Barker said. "It's not my case. It's too close to home. I only got inside here because some of the boys owed me a favour. Maybe I should have just stuck with you, Julia? Come with me."

Julia smiled her apologies to Conrad and Bella as they both began tapping on their phones at the exact same time. She hurried across the kitchen, following Barker into the grand entrance hall. The two uniformed officers guarding the front door nodded to Barker, and he nodded back.

"One of you should get on the back door," he called to them. "Someone could easily slip out. Julia, upstairs."

Julia did not argue. She let Barker practically push her up the sweeping staircase without question.

"So, *this* is her?" a forty-something man with a stubbly jaw and a crinkled suit asked when they reached the bedroom in the middle of the long hallway. "The *famous* Julia South? You're quite the celebrity at the station."

"I am?"

"Solved more murder cases than the two of us combined," the man said, folding his arms across his tight suit, looking a mixture of impressed and bitter. "Are you sure about this, boss? It's risky."

"Just keep your mouth shut, and so will I, Detective Sergeant Christie," Barker said, his hand still firmly on the bottom of Julia's back. "You know she's good."

"I know she is."

"'*She*' is still here," Julia said, looking between the two men. "What is going on here?"

"You've got a minute," DS Christie instructed, stepping back from the door. "The forensics team is on its way. You can't touch a thing."

"She knows how this works."

"How *what* works?" Julia asked, feeling like a fish out of water. "You're not seriously suggesting I – "

Before Julia could finish her sentence, Barker pushed her through the open door and into the darkened room, the only light coming from the slither of moonlight peeking through the closed curtains. She followed the silvery streak of light to Luke's wide, blank eyes.

"*Jesus!*" Julia cried, wanting to look away, but

feeling compelled to stare. "I wasn't expecting him to still be here."

"Just look around, Julia," Barker instructed, as though she was suddenly working for him. "This is my nephew. I can't be objective here. You're the best detective I've ever met, and I've worked with a lot. I'm including myself on that list."

Julia believed every word that had just left Barker's mouth, so much so, she almost forgot she was just a baker who owned a little village café.

"I stumble upon these things," she said, almost under her breath. "I talk to people, I don't inspect crime scenes."

Barker stepped back into the doorway, unable to look at his dead nephew twisted up in the sheets on the bed. It was not easy for Julia either, but Barker's encouraging words spurred her on. She knew she could do it because Barker needed her to. She had lost count of the number of bodies she had seen so far this year, but it did not make each new one any easier.

She looked at the poor boy, his bloodshot eyes staring blankly up at the ceiling. Red marks, like those of two thick hands, covered his pale neck, and his slightly parted lips were purple. He was naked, but the sheets covered his modesty. Just like when she had first met him, his phone was in his hand, and Julia was surprised his thumb was still on the button and the screen was unlocked, if not a little dim.

"Must be one of those fingerprint things," she thought aloud, leaning into the phone, knowing she could not touch a thing.

The camera application was open, the white sheets underneath reflecting through the screen. In the corner, Julia could see a tiny preview of the last picture that had been taken. She squinted, her eyesight not the best. Why was she putting off her eye test? She wanted so badly to press the picture to enlarge it, but they trusted her not to contaminate the scene. Instead, she put herself into the minds of the youngsters downstairs who always had their phones in their hands. She pulled her own out of her pocket, quickly opening the camera. She zoomed in as far as it would go, the grainy camera nowhere near as good as the one in the dead boy's hand. Regardless, she snapped a couple of pictures of the tiny preview in the corner, hoping and praying it would show something.

She pushed her phone back into her pocket, knowing she did not have time to analyse the picture yet; her minute was quickly running out. She stepped back and looked at the curtains, and then at the LED clock on the bedside table. It was not even seven in the evening yet.

"Why was he in bed?" Julia thought aloud. "And right before his uncle's surprise birthday party?"

Julia stepped back, stumbling over a bottle of lotion. Barker shot her a stern '*be careful*' look, his eyes trained on his wristwatch. She looked down at the bottle, which had spilled into a puddle on the carpet. For a moment, she thought she had been the one to knock it over, until she noticed a single boot print in the white cream. She snapped another picture, this time with her flash turned on, the white light illuminating faint footprints leading through the lotion up to the side of the bed.

"Time's up," DS Christie called into the room. "Forensics just pulled up. Get her out of there, boss."

Not needing to be told twice, Julia hurried across the room and slipped back into the bright hallway. She looked down at the picture she had just taken, pinching on the screen to zoom in on the white footprints on the dark carpet.

"*Well?*" DS Christie demanded. "Make it worth my time. I didn't find a thing in there."

"It's not that simple," Julia said. "I'm not a

clairvoyant, Detective Sergeant."

"You said she'd figure this out," DS Christie snapped, pinching between his brows, his eyes clenched. "I could lose my job over this."

"Julia?" Barker asked hopefully. "Did you find anything?"

"He took a picture on his phone," Julia offered. "It might have been before, or during the murder."

"Unless it's a close up of the killer, how's that going to help?" DS Christie snapped, clearly already exhausted with his colleague's girlfriend. "Jesus, Barker. I trusted you on this one. She can't breathe a word of this to anyone! We'll both be sacked, and Mandy has just had a baby. I can't afford to lose my job because your girlfriend is some wonder sleuth."

"You're not going to be sacked," Barker said quietly, glancing at the forensics team as they walked through the front doors. "This is on me, okay?"

"Better be."

The forensics team hurried up the stairs in their white suits, each carrying two boxes. Barker dragged Julia away from the door while DS Christie talked to them.

"He's stressed," Barker explained. "Someone broke into the post office just before this. It rattled Shilpa right up according to the officers down there.

They caught them all at the scene, so the station is rammed with processing everything. He's usually nice, I promise you."

"I'm sure he is," Julia muttered through pursed lips as she watched DS Christie drag his tie away from his neck. "Murder brings out the worst in people."

Julia pulled her phone out of her pocket and skimmed past the pictures of the carpet to the grainy and blurry photograph of the preview from Luke's phone. She turned it around, unsure of what she was looking at.

"What does that look like to you?" she asked, showing the flesh coloured blur to Barker.

"A bottom," he said, tilting his head and grabbing the phone from Julia. "A very round bottom. I think so, at least. There's a curve there that looks like one."

"You think?" Julia asked, taking the phone back, not as convinced. "You need to pass on the message that they need to check it out. And there are footprints in there. They might belong to the killer."

Barker nodded, his eyes distant as he stared down at the lavish glittering chandelier hanging over the entrance. Julia slid her hands softly around his waist and pulled him into a tight hug.

"I'm sorry," she whispered, the guilt rising up again. "I'm so sorry this has happened."

"It's not your fault," Barker said. "We need to figure this out."

"We will."

"Tonight."

"*Tonight*?" Julia echoed, her voice catching in her throat as she pulled away from his chest. "How?"

"DS Christie, is the station still packed?" Barker called across the landing to the DS who was talking on the phone.

"They've just brought in a bunch of kids who stole a car over on the Fern Moore Estate," he cried, rolling his eyes as his jaw gritted tightly. "What's happening in this village tonight? Is there a full moon?"

Barker tapped his finger against his chin as he looked down at the carpet running down the hallway, nodding as though a plan was forming in his mind.

"Okay, John," Barker called to the DS. "Cordon this place off. No one comes in or out. I want all of the officers we can get circling the perimeter, and I want a road block put in place for the lane. Julia, can you gather everyone in the living-room? It's time I faced my family."

"Are you sure that's wise, boss?" DS Christie asked, his voice softening. "The victim is your nephew, and you're not on duty. You'll be going rogue."

"Are you going to snitch on me, DS Christie?"

"Of course not, boss."

"Then as of now, I *am* on duty. You said it yourself, the station is rammed and we just don't have the resources available right now. Once forensics are out of here, they'll take my nephew away, and it'll be sunrise before anything else official happens, and it might be too late by then. We're cracking this tonight." Barker paused, clasping his hands over Julia's shoulders. "A member of my family killed Luke, and I'm not leaving until I'm dragging them out of here in handcuffs. You don't have to help, but I think we'll get there a lot sooner if you do."

"I wasn't going to give you a choice, Barker Brown," Julia said, ignoring the excited gurgle in her stomach at the prospect of working alongside Barker on a case. "We'll figure this out."

CHAPTER 5

Barker paced up and down in front of the fireplace underneath his giant '*HAPPY BIRTHDAY BARKER*!' banner. Balloons branded with the message scattered the room, the thickest concentration surrounding the buffet table in front of the large windows on the far side of the room. Untouched silver foil covered the twenty or so different plates.

Casper and Heather were sitting on one couch, with Bella and Conrad standing behind them. Theo lingered by the drinks cabinet, his arms folded across his chest. His identical twin, Ethan, was on the opposite side of the room in front of the buffet table, staring blankly at the floor, his face pale and eyes red. Dawn sobbed into his chest, only highlighting the deafening silence that had fallen on the room when Barker had strode in.

"How has this happened?" Heather asked, a tissue pressed against her nose, her free hand clasped around her husband's. "It doesn't make any sense."

Barker continued to pace, every muscle in his face tight as he concentrated on his thoughts. Julia had not seen him so tense before.

"One of you did this," Barker said suddenly without stopping. "One of you killed Luke."

"Barker –" Casper started.

"You all come here, and he's killed within twenty-four hours," Barker snapped, turning to face his family, making sure to look each of them in the eyes, except for Ethan and Dawn who seemed to be somewhere else entirely. "It's not a coincidence, Casper."

"Why would any of us want to kill him?" Bella said through her sniffles. "You sound crazy, Uncle

Barker."

Julia smiled her support across the room at Barker, but he was too deep in thought to notice.

"I'm going to interview each of you," he said, looking around the room again. "I don't expect you all to tell the truth, in fact, I expect the opposite."

"Is that *really* necessary?" Theo asked, forcing a laugh and stepping forward to join his daughter. "None of us did it. We weren't the only ones in this house, Barker."

"So, you're suggesting a heavily pregnant woman strangled him?" Barker replied, his eyes narrowing on his older brother. "Or what about Julia's father, who only met the kid yesterday afternoon?"

Theo opened his mouth to reply, but no words came out. He wrapped his hand around Bella's shoulder, pulling her away from her boyfriend, who looked just as dumbfounded as he had in the kitchen.

"Julia, can you tell your father to prepare his study?" Barker asked, finally looking at her. "I'm going to start right away."

Julia turned on her heels and headed for the foot of the stairs, leaving Barker in the frosty silence with his family.

When she reached the top of the stairs, she crept

along the hallway to the master bedroom. She had no idea if this was where her father would be, but she had a good idea it was where Katie would be.

"*What?*" Katie's shrill voice cried out after Julia knocked. "What do you want?"

Julia twisted the firm doorknob and crept into the dimly lit room. Katie was in the centre of the mammoth bed, her large bump jutting up towards the canopy draped over the four-poster frame surrounding her. Brian was perched on the edge of the bed, one hand wrapped around Katie's and the other rubbing the deep creases across his forehead.

"Julia," Katie said, a little more softly, able to muster a smile. "How did you get in here? They're keeping us as prisoners!"

"I snuck in," she confessed as she approached Katie's side of the bed, the crystal beaded lamp on her bedside table barely enough to light the entire room. "How are you feeling?"

"Confused," Katie responded, her makeup-covered face looking a little worse for wear after the events of the last hour. "I found him. I thought it was so rude that he was choosing to sleep, and well – I guess he wasn't sleeping, after all."

Julia grabbed Katie's free hand, and the two women shared a rare moment of genuine connection. The last thing Julia wanted was for Katie's stress levels to rise, especially so close to her due date.

"It's bringing back awful memories," Katie said, her acrylic nails digging into Julia's palm. "It's reminding me of when that boy pushed my brother, Charles, out of the window, and you and Barker thought I'd done it!"

"That was a long time ago," Brian reminded her. "We've moved past that."

"I know, I know," Katie said, shaking her head and disrupting her blonde curls. "It's not fair for us. Why *our* house? Daddy is shaken up!"

Katie let go of Julia's hand and pointed into the corner of the room. Julia followed her finger, her heart jumping when she noticed Vincent Wellington sitting silently in the corner of the room in his wheelchair. He stared blankly at the carpet as he always did. If he was aware of what was happening in his house, he had no way of expressing it. Julia glanced at her father, who could only offer a slight shrug as a way of explanation.

"Did anything happen today?" Julia asked, edging closer to Katie. "Anything that might have prompted this?"

"Today has been pretty quiet," Brian said. "But

last night was a different story."

"What happened?"

"Hilary spent all night cooking a lovely dinner for everyone. I invited the whole family to the dining room for the meal, but only Casper and Heather showed up. Ethan and Dawn ordered Chinese and ate it in their room. I didn't even see Luke until earlier today. He was digging around in the kitchen looking for some beer. I gave him a couple of cans to take up to his room because I knew he wouldn't be coming out. He was constantly tapping away on that phone of his the whole time I was trying to talk to him."

"And that's when I heard Heather arguing with Luke," Katie jumped in, looking at her husband to let him know she was going to take over. "I was in the bathroom on the landing because our en suite toilet isn't flushing properly. I was drying my hands when I heard raised voices. It's my house, so I had every right to listen in. I emptied out the toothbrush holder and placed it against the door. I saw it in a movie, and it actually worked!" Katie paused, giggling proudly at her method of eavesdropping. "I could tell it was Luke because of that London accent. He said something about an app, and then Heather snapped back something about money."

"That's when I came upstairs," Brian said. "They scattered and went into their own bedrooms, and we didn't see them again until this morning."

"They were arguing about an app?" Julia asked, scratching the side of her head. "Like a phone app?"

"It could have been an apple," Katie said with a shrug. "But why would they be arguing about an apple?"

"Why would they be arguing about an app?" Julia thought aloud. "How strange. There was definitely tension coming from Casper and Heather when they saw Luke yesterday."

"They're a strange family," Katie said. "Barker seems like the only normal one."

"And Casper," Brian said firmly. "Casper is a good man."

Suddenly remembering what Barker had asked her to do, Julia relayed the information to her father. He did not seem too happy about letting them use his study, but he left the room all the same.

"Did anything happen in the run up to the murder?"

"I didn't see anyone who arrived yesterday until it was almost time for the party," Katie said. "There was a lot of slamming doors, and raised voices, but nothing I could make out. Theo and his daughter arrived with that handsome boy this afternoon. Bella, I think she's called. She's lovely. She said she'd promote my fake tan brand when I get it off the ground."

"For a small fee?"

"She said she'd give me a family discount," Katie said excitedly. "She has eleven thousand followers!"

"Conrad has one hundred thousand," Julia repeated the fact like she understood what it meant. "What did they do all day?"

"They took pictures, mostly," Katie said, scrunching up her nose as she thought back. "Bella said it was the perfect place for a photo shoot. They took their pictures on their phones. It was nothing like my modelling days."

Katie nodded to the canvasses lining the walls, more of her body on show than Julia was comfortable with seeing.

"It seems to be their thing," Julia said. "It's Conrad's job, apparently."

"Taking pictures of himself?" Katie asked arching a brow, making Julia glad she was not the only one who did not really understand. "He *is* very handsome."

"He is," Julia found herself saying before she even thought about it. "A little self-involved, if you ask me."

"The good looking ones usually are," Katie said with a shrug as she tossed her peroxide hair over her shoulder. "Can you pass me my handbag? I need a touch-up. My T-zone is an oily mess. I want to look my best if they're going to take another mug shot."

"You're going to be fine," Julia said, reaching down to pass Katie her black designer handbag. "Unless you did it?"

"I don't think I could if I wanted to," she said, pointing at the large bump with a giggle. "I haven't seen my toes in months, and I can barely carry anything over five pounds."

"Will you be okay on your own?"

"I'm not alone," Katie said, nodding at her father as she dug through her extensive collection of makeup. "Daddy is here."

Leaving Katie to powder her nose and reapply her lipstick, Julia slipped out of the bedroom, the bright lights of the hallway blinding her.

She walked down the hallway towards the bathroom, needing a moment to herself, the image of Luke's poor body still etched in her mind. She almost felt bad for thinking that she disliked the boy yesterday; she had not even known him.

Walking past his bedroom, which had been

cordoned off by the forensics team as they went over the room with a fine toothcomb, she opened the bathroom door and slipped inside. She rested her head on the cold wood, her eyes closed; it felt nice to be alone.

"Can I help you?" a deep male voice asked.

Julia's eyes sprung open, the discovery that she was not alone hitting her full force. She parted her lips to speak as she stared ahead at the bald man, who she first thought was Ethan, but quickly realised was Theo when she saw his straight nose in the mirror's reflection.

"We haven't officially met," Julia said, stretching out a hand and taking a step forward. "I'm Julia. Barker's girlfriend."

"That's all very well and good, but I was in here first," Theo snapped, his dark brows, the only thing to remind her of Barker, low over his eyes. "Don't you know how to knock?"

Julia looked down at her hand before dropping it to her side. She could not blame the man for being angry. Even though he was only leaning against the sink, it could have been a lot worse.

"I'm sorry," she said, taking a tentative step back. "It's been a very odd day."

"You're telling me," Theo mumbled as he

turned back to the mirror. "These damn things are irritating me."

He pulled down the skin under his eyes, his pupils drifting up into the back of his head. He blinked hard with his finger pressed against his eyeball, something slimy and small coming away on the tip.

"Contact lenses don't mix when you keep crying," he admitted in a deep voice, the corners of his mouth pricking into a sad smile as he caught Julia's gaze in the reflection. "I wasn't that close to my nephew, but he was too young to die. I think our family is cursed."

"I'm sorry for your loss," Julia offered pathetically, looking back at the door, wishing she had knocked after all. "This isn't how I wanted us all to meet."

"I wasn't even going to come," he said. "After what happened with Bethany I – never mind. Bella convinced me to come. Well, it was Conrad, really. He wanted to take some pictures in the countryside. He said it would be good for his '*layout*'."

"Layout?"

"His online gallery," Theo said with a shake of his head to let Julia know they were on the same page when it came to the understanding of the language the younger ones were speaking. "He said some greenery would break up the urban backdrops. I don't know. He's brought a case load of clothes that he's being paid to advertise. I'd rather he got a real job, but he's making more money than most kids his age. They were going to shoot tomorrow before we left, but – we weren't expecting this."

"None of us were," Julia said, sighing heavily as she thought about the birthday cake she had spent so long baking, which was at risk of spoiling in the boot of her car. "I should get back. Sorry for intruding."

"It's okay," he said, turning back to the mirror to take out his second contact lens. "You were right. It is a shame we're meeting under these circumstances."

Julia slipped out of the bathroom, leaving Theo alone. The second she left him, she heard the soft sobs of a grieving uncle on the other side of the door.

"Julia?" her father called up the stairs, a cup in his hand. "I've made you some of that peppermint and liquorice tea you like. I bought some specially."

Never happier to see her father, Julia padded softly down the staircase, a cup of her favourite tea just what she needed.

CHAPTER 6

By the time Julia finished her tea it was almost eight in the evening. It somehow felt much later, but Julia decided she would switch to coffee to fend off exhaustion if needed. If Barker was staying awake all night to figure out what had happened, Julia would too.

After washing her cup and placing it on the metal draining board, she looked through the cupboards before moving onto the large pantry, jealous that she did not have one in her small cottage. Despite no one in the house being bakers, they seemed to own every ingredient to make anything Julia's heart could have desired. She did not realise she was gathering the things to make her mother's chocolate chip cookies until her arms were almost full. Kicking the pantry door back into its frame, she walked carefully over to the island and placed down the ingredients, careful not to knock over the open bag of flour.

Baking was Julia's chosen form of therapy; it was free, if you did not include the cost of ingredients, which she did not, especially when she was baking in someone else's kitchen.

Julia was not stupid; she knew her baking served a double purpose. As she measured out the flour, she made sure to pour enough for everyone in the house to have at least four cookies each if they wanted, including the officers and DS Christie. A sugary, buttery chocolate chip cookie could do things that hours of interrogation could not.

By the time Julia carefully placed the finished warm cookies onto a cooling rack, two men walked past the kitchen door carrying a stretcher, a black body bag lying motionlessly on top. Out of respect,

Julia averted her eyes, but the shrill cry of a bereaved mother made her eyes drift up.

Across the entrance hall in the arms of her husband, Dawn screamed, her strawberry blonde hair flailing across her face, her arms outstretched towards her son as he made his way to the ambulance, which would drive away without a siren. Julia looked down at her cookies, knowing this was beyond even her baking skills.

Barker opened the door to the study, DS Christie right behind him. Casper hobbled out, his lips snarled, and his head low. He paused, leaning against his cane before turning back to face Barker. The two men looked nothing like each other, but from the look of shared disappointment on each of their faces, they could not be anything but brothers.

"*Cookies?*" a sharp voice cried, coming from a second door on the other side of the kitchen. "You've baked *cookies?*"

Julia turned to see Hilary, the housekeeper, walking carefully across the kitchen, her short heels clicking on the polished tiles. Her wiry blonde and grey hair was pulled back into a snug bun on the top of her head as usual, and her eyes were lined with charcoal liner just like every other time Julia had seen her. Her grey cardigan was creaseless, her skirt perfectly pleated, her shoes matte, and scuff-free.

"I hope you don't mind," Julia said, pushing the cooling rack towards Hilary. "I think they're best when they're still a little warm. Makes the chocolate gooey."

Hilary looked down at the cookies, and then up at Julia as though she had just been offered something illegal. Without responding, she marched over to the mess Julia had stacked carefully in the sink for washing later.

"I'll sort that out," Julia said quickly, stepping in Hilary's path. "Why don't you sit down?"

"I don't clock off until nine," she said firmly, her back stiffening as she checked the small watch on the inside of her wrist. "Been the same way for forty years."

"And tonight, a boy was murdered in his bed," Julia said, offering a seat at the island. "Sit down and have a cookie. No one is going to mind."

Hilary stared at the dishes in the sink, her bulbous eyes bulging out of their sockets. To Julia's surprise, the stiff housekeeper took the offer of a seat. She looked so uncomfortable perching on the edge, one foot still on the floor, her hands clasped in her lap, Julia wondered if she had ever sat at the island before. Julia picked up one of the cookies and took a bite, the warm chocolate making her mouth water the second it hit her tongue. She pushed the cooling rack across to Hilary, who reached out and plucked one from the side, her eyes darting down to the crumbs on the counter.

"This is rather good," Hilary said in a surprised tone after her first bite. "Very nice indeed."

"I've never seen you in my café," Julia said, pulling up a seat next to Hilary. "In fact, I don't think I've ever seen you in the village."

"I don't get down much," she replied. "I work a lot. I get my supplies from the supermarket out of town."

"Doesn't that get boring?"

"I love cleaning," she said, pausing to take another bite. "You're a skilled baker."

"Thank you," Julia said, the smile on her face genuine. "And you're a skilled cleaner. You put my cottage to shame."

A tiny smile prickled Hilary's tight lips; Julia considered that it was the first she had seen grace the grumpy woman's face.

"I saw him," Hilary said after finishing the last piece of cookie. "The boy. I ran over when I heard Katie scream. I was doing a crossword in my bedroom before the party started. I'd been cooking all day, so I was taking a little break." Hilary paused, her expression souring. "They say you look like you're sleeping when you die, but he didn't. He looked scared."

"He did," Julia agreed, a lump rising in her throat. "I think I would too if someone strangled me. It's one of the few ways to kill someone where you have to actually *look* in the victim's eyes. Also, one of the few ways that is truly spontaneous."

"Spontaneous?"

"It means they didn't plan it."

"I *know* what the word means, child," Hilary snapped, her frosty edges prickling up again. "I just always thought murders had to be meticulously planned."

"Some are," Julia said with a nod, her eyes fixed on the cookies, her stomach rumbling. "But strangling is so immediate and primal. There are easier ways to kill without it being obvious."

"You seem to know a lot."

"I keep getting tangled up in these things," Julia said, pushing her hands up into her curly hair, dreaming of the day she could go a full month without another body springing up. "I think I've had more column inches in *The Peridale Post* this year than most people will in a lifetime."

"I don't read it," Hilary admitted, offering a shrug. "It's no different than a tabloid rag. Why do I care about flower shows and club meetings? I'm happy to keep myself to myself up here."

"Probably for the best," Julia said, glancing to the study as Barker led Heather inside for questioning. "Although it seems tonight the action has come to you, and I can't help but feel responsible for that."

"As you should," Hilary said firmly with a measured nod. "Although you should not feel guilty for the boy's murder. He died at the hands of one of his family members. My guess would be that whatever drove that person to kill would have happened whether they were here, or wherever they came from."

"Perhaps you're right," Julia said, hoping that was the case. "Although they're from different parts of the country."

Hilary considered Julia's words for a moment. To her surprise, Hilary reached out for a second cookie; Julia did the same.

"These *really* are nice," Hilary said, her eyes focussing on the rough surface. "You were right about them being pleasant when warm. You can really taste the butter. People are afraid to use it these days. Everything will kill you if you believe the news." Hilary lifted the rest of the cookie up to her lips before pulling it back down and dropping it onto the white marble counter. "Being a housekeeper means you get very good at being invisible. You learn to know when you should be seen, and when you need to vanish in an instant. They haven't even thought to interview me yet. Perhaps they're getting to me, but I suspect I've slipped their minds. I doubt they even know I'm here."

Julia crammed the rest of her cookie into her mouth as she stared at Hilary. When she realised what Hilary was implying, Julia almost choked on the crumbs as she hurried to swallow them.

"Do you know something?" Julia asked, her eyes popping out of her head to match Hilary's. "Tell me."

"I would never have said anything if the boy wasn't currently en route to a hospital morgue," Hilary said, pointing her finger at Julia. "I want you to know that. Another part of being a housekeeper is knowing when to keep your mouth shut. What people get up to after dark has nothing to do with me."

"After dark?"

"The sun sets rather early this time of year, doesn't it?" Hilary said. "I always thought it was funny how people choose to do these things under the cover of darkness, but I presume they feel safer. They would have been better waiting until the early hours of the morning if they really wanted to go unseen, although I expect there would be no fun in it, would there?"

"Fun in what?" Julia begged, edging closer and closer. "What did you see, Hilary?"

"The sun set on Peridale Manor around half past four today," Hilary said. "I saw the handsome blond man enter Luke's bedroom at five."

"*Conrad?*"

"He didn't leave until twenty-five minutes later, and he was in a state of undress."

"Undress?" Julia asked. "You mean –"

"Let's just say the young man has a very chiselled torso and toned thighs," Hilary said, blushing a little as she slid off the stool. "I was dusting the skirting boards, I was not spying. Either way, the boy didn't see me."

"You're saying Luke was having an affair with *Conrad?*" Julia asked, her eyes popping open even wider. "An affair with his cousin's boyfriend?"

"I told you what I saw," Hilary said, picking up

three more of the cookies and slotting them into the pocket of her cardigan. "I think I will enjoy the rest in my room. Do with my information what you please, Julia. Just stay out of trouble. We've had enough death in the manor this year. I'd like to see in the New Year without another ghost stalking the hallways."

Julia promised that she would try her best to stay out of trouble. She let out a disbelieving laugh as she watched Hilary leave the way she had entered. She felt like a fool for not even considering the housekeeper. Julia pulled her phone from her pocket and looked at the grainy picture she had taken of Luke's mobile phone. She pinched the screen and zoomed in, turning the phone upside down. Had Barker been right? Was she staring at someone's behind?

A rattle at the window made Julia drop her phone onto the counter with a clatter. She jumped out of her seat, her breath short, heart racing. Just as Bella had a few hours ago with her, Julia turned to see Jessie cupping her hands against the window.

"Let me in," Jessie whispered. "I've just had to dodge two police officers."

"What are you doing here?" Julia cried, hurrying across the kitchen. "It's not safe."

"I'm bored," she huffed. "Dot is forcing me to play word association, and she keeps ending up on '*aubergine*'. Even when we're playing an animal round, it always goes back to the bloody aubergines."

"You've been out there this whole time?" Julia asked, not knowing why she was surprised; she should not have expected any less. "It's freezing!"

"Neil picked Sue up an hour ago," Jessie said, her hot breath steaming up the glass. "Dot made him bring a thermos of tea, a blanket, a tin of shortbread, and a radio. I can't bear to watch her suck another piece of shortbread while she mumbles the words to The Beatles. Let me in, Julia. I'm cold."

Jessie pouted like a little girl, her red nose pressed up against the glass, her eyes similar to Mowgli's when he wanted feeding; Julia could not bring herself to say no to that face.

"Five minutes," Julia said after unlocking the door. "You can't be here."

"Why not?" Jessie said, a grin spreading from ear to ear as she slipped through the gap. "There's no way I'm going back to the aubergine game."

"Where does she think you are?"

"Told her I was going to pee in a bush," Jessie said with a shrug as she looked around the kitchen.

"Did you bake cookies?"

Jessie immediately crammed one into her mouth, followed closely by a second.

"*S'good*," she said, wet crumbs flying everywhere.

"How did you get past the patrol officers?" Julia asked, casting an eye to the patio doors as one of the officers walked past, tipping his head to Julia, not noticing that Jessie was someone entirely new.

"I used to be homeless," Jessie said as though it were obvious. "It was my job to hide from the police. So, what's the score? Found the strangler yet?"

Jessie climbed up onto the seat Hilary had been sat in. She crammed another cookie into her mouth, spilling golden crumbs down the front of her black hoody.

"What does this look like to you?" Julia asked, picking up her phone to show Jessie. "Barker thinks it looks like –"

"It's a big butt," Jessie said, barely pausing for breath before grabbing a fourth cookie. "Who sent you their butt?"

"Nobody *sent* it," Julia said, pulling the cooling rack away. "I need those. I didn't bake enough for you."

"As your bribes go, they're pretty delicious."

"They're not bribes," Julia said with a dry smirk. "More like lip softeners. And I got the picture from the victim's phone. It was on the screen, but it was only a tiny preview. This is the best photograph I could get."

"So it's his butt?" Jessie asked, her eyes firmly on the cookies as her brows tensed together. "That's a bit sick. Who takes a picture of their butt?"

"It might be someone else's," Julia whispered, turning to the grand entrance hall as Bella and Conrad wandered into the sitting room hand in hand. "I have a lead I want to follow up on."

"Follow away," Jessie said, diving across the counter to snatch up another cookie. "I'll just stay here. If anyone comes, I'll pretend I don't speak English. That was always my favourite trick. *No comprende, Mister Police*."

Julia slid the remaining cookies onto a large plate, leaving Jessie in the kitchen. Julia did not care that she was now four cookies short, it was just nice to see Jessie back to her old self again.

"I wish I'd known all it would take was a murder to cheer her up," Julia whispered to herself as she walked across the grand entrance towards the sitting room to question Conrad about what he was doing in Luke's bedroom.

CHAPTER 7

"*Julia*!" a voice hissed across the entrance hall, stopping her in her tracks before she reached the sitting room. "Would you be able to help an old man out?"

Through the gap in the door to the downstairs bathroom, Julia could see Casper sitting on the toilet. She almost turned away, not wanting another situation like when she had interrupted Theo. When she noticed that his trousers were pulled up and fastened, she felt safe to look.

"How can I help, Casper?" Julia asked, resting her plate of cookies on a side table next to the sitting room archway.

"I've been a bit of a fool," he said, his shaky smile fluttering the moustache on his top lip. "I decided I was going to be stubborn and go to the bathroom alone while Heather was being interviewed. I wanted to keep my dignity and not ask for help, but, well – I've been sitting here for fifteen minutes, and I just *can't* seem to get up. I've got so used to our high toilets with handles on either side, I'd forgotten how low the rest of the world did their business."

Julia pulled back the door. Casper's cane was on the floor next to the bath. She picked it up and rested it against the wall before pulling Casper up with both hands. He was even heavier than he looked, so it took three attempts for Julia to get the man steady on his feet. When he was finally vertical, he motioned for Julia to pass him his cane. As though he felt naked without it, an easy smile filled his face when it was back by his side for support.

"Let's not talk about this, eh?" he asked with a wink, his cheeks blushing. "A one-legged old man doesn't have much dignity to begin with, but I'd like to keep the last shred I have."

"Consider it our secret," Julia whispered. "Would you like a chocolate chip cookie?"

Casper's face lit up, letting her know he would like one very much. They walked out of the small bathroom with Julia holding his arm to steady him. He smiled at her to let her know it was not necessary, so she let go to scoop up the plate.

"I'm a nervous baker," she explained. "I couldn't help myself."

"If it's what helps you cope," he said as he circled his finger above the cookies before choosing one of the thicker ones. "We all have our vices. I suppose mine is food too, but not making it, eating it. Truth be told, I'm a terrible cook. I don't know what I'd do without Heather."

They drifted across to the foot of the stairs and sat down, the plate of cookies between them. Julia could tell Casper was in pain, even if he was trying to hide it behind a tight smile. She offered him another cookie, which he accepted gratefully.

"I'm not used to wearing this damn thing," he said, slapping the fake leg, which produced an unnatural echo inside his trouser leg. "I've got used to hobbling around at home with a crutch. I've even got quite fast at it, but I wouldn't feel right legless in front of people. That's pride for you."

"It must be difficult for you."

"It happened a long time ago," he said, hiking up the bottom of his trousers to flash Julia some of the prosthetic leg. "You'd think I'd be used to it by now, but I still wake up every morning with pain in the foot I haven't had for thirty-five years. The Falklands War was quick, but it was brutal. I was lucky to walk away with just a missing leg compared to some of my pals. People are a lot more accepting of folk like me these days. I thank the Paralympics for that, but people never truly understand the pain. Forcing a stump down on a fake leg hurts, Julia. It hurts a lot, and I'm an old man. I should have been asleep an hour ago, but how can I sleep when my nephew has just died? I'm not going to lie and say we've been close recently because we haven't, but he's still flesh and blood."

"I sensed there was some tension yesterday."

"Was it that obvious?" he replied with a sad chuckle. "It all seems so silly now, but he wasn't an easy man to love. We gave him some money a while ago, and he –"

Before he could finish his sentence, the door to the study opened. Heather shuffled out, her plump face low as she fiddled with a paper napkin. Barker smiled sadly down at her as she hobbled across the hall to her husband.

"Are you eating cookies, Casper Brown?" Heather cried, her voice lacking the warmth it had contained when Julia had first met her. "You know you shouldn't have snacks after eight."

"It's the stress, Heather," he insisted, forcing himself up using the bannister and his cane. "I was just telling Julia about how we gave Luke that money for –"

"Why are you telling *her* that?" she snapped, her beady eyes widening like saucers. "She doesn't need to know the personal details of our life!"

"She's family."

"Family, or not, it's nobody's business," Heather insisted, looping her arm through her husband's. "No offence, Julia, but we don't know you from Eve."

Julia nodded her understanding, and watched as Heather and Casper walked slowly towards the sitting room. Julia scooped up the cookies, hanging back for a moment before following them. She stood in the archway of the sitting room, but Conrad and Bella were nowhere to be seen.

"*Julia?*" Barker's voice travelled from the study

doorway. "Are you busy?"

"Not anymore."

Once in the dimly lit study, Julia placed the plate on the desk where the tape recorder had been set up. DS Christie immediately grabbed one, but Barker hung back.

"What have you got?" Julia asked.

"That's classified," DS Christie said quickly, crumbs flying out of his mouth. "Good biscuits. Where they from?"

"I made them," Julia said. "Technically, it's a cookie. It's softer and bigger than a biscuit."

"Aren't they the same thing?" DS Christie replied, narrowing his eyes on Julia.

"Sort of," Julia said with a shrug. "It's not important right now. What do you have?"

"It's still classified."

"Leave off, John," Barker said, rubbing between his eyes. "She wouldn't be asking unless she knew something useful too."

DS Christie collapsed into the chair and picked up another cookie. He pulled off his already loose tie and tossed it across the bookcase-lined room.

"Was Luke gay?" Julia asked in a low voice.

"I don't know," Barker replied. "I haven't seen him for three years."

"Since Bethany's funeral?" Julia asked.

"How do you know about Bethany?" he asked sharply. "I never told you about her."

"No, but her name has come up a dozen times in the past two days," she said, turning her back on DS Christie to lean against the thick mahogany desk. "She seems to be an important part of your family history, but we'll come back to that. I think Conrad and Luke were having an affair."

"*What*?" DS Christie scoffed, choking on a cookie. "Conrad has a girlfriend."

"So?"

"Well, he's not – ya'know. Like *that*."

"Gay?" Julia snapped, craning her neck to face the DS. "You can say it, you know. It's not catching." She turned back to Barker and folded her arms. "I have it from a *very* reliable source that Conrad was seen going into Luke's room at five, and leaving twenty-five minutes later in a '*state of undress*'. Unless they were playing strip poker, I think that speaks for itself."

Barker picked up a notepad from the table, where he had cobbled together a crude timeline.

"Seems to check out," he said over her shoulder to DS Christie. "According to your father, Theo, Luke, Bella, Conrad, Casper, and Heather were all in the sitting room around four in the evening. Luke complained about a headache around quarter to five and said he was going up for a nap before the party. Conrad and Bella went for a walk around the grounds five minutes later, but Bella returned around five past the hour saying that Conrad was taking a work call."

"And he was really in bed with his girlfriend's cousin?" DS Christie asked, a little less sceptically this time. "Your family is messed up, even by my standards, and two of my cousins married each other!"

Julia found herself on the same page as the DS. Ever since meeting Ethan, Dawn and Luke at the train station, she had felt her perception of the Brown family shattering piece by piece.

"Brian said everyone left the sitting room by half past five, and forensics is estimating the time of death as being between half past five and six, meaning he was likely killed immediately before Katie discovered him."

"Not officially, though," DS Christie jumped in. "We won't know for sure until the autopsy, but that will take days."

"So, it could still be any of them?" Julia asked, frustrated that they had not narrowed down the list of suspects. "We're getting nowhere."

"Go and find Theo," Barker said to DS Christie after checking his list. "I need a break. Let's go for a walk, Julia."

Julia did not argue. She followed Barker out of the study, taking her cookies with her, much to DS Christie's displeasure. She walked quickly into the kitchen and placed them on the counter, not surprised in the least to see that Jessie had wandered off.

"I need some air," Barker said. "This place is suffocating me."

"I thought we couldn't go outside?"

"We're not suspects," he reminded her. "We're probably the only two people in this manor with concrete alibis, aside from John, your father, and Katie."

"And Jessie," Julia said. "She's wandering around in there somewhere. Don't ask."

To her surprise, Barker did not ask. They walked through the front doors, nodding to the officer on duty. The night was cold, probably only a couple of degrees above freezing. Even though the bitter chill nipped at Julia's exposed skin, she was glad of the fresh air. Barker pulled off his jacket and draped it over her shoulders.

"I should have told you everything before it got to this," Barker said, looping his arm through hers as they walked past her Ford Anglia where Dot was fast asleep behind the wheel, a blanket bundled around her head. "It's not that I lied to you, it's just been a complicated mess for a while now. I didn't even know how to explain it."

"Since Bethany's death?"

"Before that," Barker said with a heavy sigh as they walked around the side of the house. "Since Mum died five years ago. She was the glue holding us together. We'd gather at her house, and it kept us close. Birthdays, Mother's Day, Christmases, Easter. No matter what we were doing, we'd *always* be there, for her mainly, but we also enjoyed using it as a way to catch up. Now, it's a Christmas card and birthday phone calls, if I'm lucky. I didn't even notice that this was the first year none of them called me, but now I know why."

"And Bethany?"

"Bethany was my niece," Barker explained as they walked through the bubble of light streaming out of the kitchen. "Theo's eldest daughter. Bella's older sister. She would have been twenty-one last month. She was only eighteen when she died. It was no age for her to go."

"How did it happen?"

"She was drunk behind the wheel." He paused to inhale deeply. "We all gathered for her eighteenth birthday three years ago. It was the first time we had properly all been together since Mum's funeral. We all had a great time. We always got on as well as brothers did.

"At the end of the night, Bethany decided she was going to drive home. None of us knew. We didn't even know she'd been drinking. She just slipped away from the party and got into her car. Ethan got in too. They were staying at the same hotel. He was drunk. Too drunk to notice that she was also drunk, or so we all suspect. We don't blame him, well, all of us except for Theo. He said outright at the funeral that he blamed Ethan for his daughter's death and vowed never to speak to him again. That's why I'm so surprised you got them to agree to come here."

"Theo was the difficult one," Julia said. "He told me he only came because Conrad wanted to come and take pictures. I wonder if Conrad really wanted to come because he knew Luke would be here? On the morning I picked Luke up from the train station with his mum and dad, he asked me specifically if Bella would be bringing Conrad. It all makes sense now."

"When you asked if I thought Luke was gay, I didn't want to answer in front of John in case he repeated something back to Ethan and Dawn. The last thing they need now is to find out something like this when he has only been dead a couple of hours. I babysat him when he was about fourteen. He was different back then. This was before his job took over. I let him go on my computer, and I found some stuff after. I don't think he knew how to clear the history. He was only typing in questions. I remember one of them was '*will people still like me if I am gay?*' I never brought it up."

"What did he do for a job?"

"He developed apps," Barker said. "Ran a big shot company in London. They made games and things like that for phones."

"So, it *was* apps, not apples," Julia said, almost to herself. "That makes more sense."

"Apples?" Barker asked, forcing a laugh. "What are you talking about?"

"Katie overheard Heather and Luke arguing on the landing last night about money and apps."

"Oh," Barker said, suddenly standing still. "She didn't mention that in her statement."

"Casper was about to tell me about some money

they had given to Luke, but Heather shut him down and basically said she didn't trust me."

"Well, she must not trust me either," Barker said quietly. "She's known me since I was born. Mum had Casper when she was sixteen, and she had me when she was forty-five. She was an old mother in those days, but she never cared. I've always been closest with Casper, even though Theo and Ethan are only three years older than me."

"Ethan said you all had different fathers."

"We do," Barker said with a nod. "Except Ethan and Theo, of course. Casper's dad died when he was a child, and the twins' dad left while she was pregnant with them. I never knew mine. Mum never wanted to speak about it, so I didn't ask. I loved her too much to upset her, and she loved us. That's why we all have her maiden name, Brown, rather than our fathers' names. She wanted us all to belong, and it worked until she died, but look at us now. I'm questioning them about a murder, and I *know* someone in my family did it, and now I know that at least two of them are lying to me about money."

"It might not be connected," Julia suggested.

"That's not the point," Barker said. "A hallway argument is the sort of thing you bring up in an interview unless you have something to hide."

Julia could not object; the logic seemed spot on. She was good at talking to people on a human level, but she knew nothing about official interviewing techniques. She took people at face value most of the time, using a combination of her wits and her own logic patterns, which more often than not led her to the solution.

"I still need to talk to Ethan and Dawn," Barker said when they reached the front of the house again. "I wanted to give them some space to come to terms with it, but they might know something."

They walked back inside, the entrance hall wrapping around her frozen skin like a warm blanket. She shrugged off the jacket and handed it back to Barker, who accepted it before heading back to the study. Julia turned to the kitchen to grab her cookies, but what she saw was an empty plate and Jessie with chocolate around her mouth.

CHAPTER 8

Julia bolted up in an armchair, a heavy blanket over her, and the warmth of the roaring fire prickling her cheek. She turned to Jessie who was sitting cross-legged on the couch staring at her.

"I fell asleep?" Julia croaked, not remembering crawling under a blanket. "How long have I been out?"

"It's almost midnight," Jessie said, pulling back

her hood a little before stuffing her hands into her hoody pocket. "I put the blanket over you. Barker lit the fire."

"*Midnight?*" Julia cried, jumping up. "Why didn't you wake me?"

"Because you must have needed it, cake lady," Jessie said. "Don't worry. I've been sitting here keeping watch. Your neck was safe."

Julia lifted her hand up to her neck, not believing she had fallen asleep on the job. She thought back to walking into the sitting room with Jessie, disappointed to find it empty. She had sat down for a moment, and the last thing she remembered was chatting to Jessie about her baking course at college.

"Has anything happened?" Julia asked, cracking her stiff neck.

"Nope," Jessie said with a shrug as she let out a yawn. "Barker is interviewing Ethan. I think he's the last one. Haven't seen anyone since we came in here."

"Why don't you go home and get some sleep?"

"I'm not leaving you."

"I'll be fine," Julia insisted. "I'm a big girl."

"So am I," Jessie said, jumping up and forcing down another yawn. "I'm not leaving you when there's a strangler on the loose."

"I'll be fine," Julia repeated.

"You're poking your nose into other people's business and asking a lot of questions," Jessie said with a roll of her eyes. "If I were a murderer, I'd be cracking my knuckles ready to choke the life out of you."

Julia's hand drifted up to her neck again. As usual, she had not considered that she was jumping into harm's way by investigating another murder case.

"I think we're safe," Julia said. "I think the murder was spontaneous."

"Spontaneous?"

"It means they didn't –"

"I know what it means, Julia," Jessie snapped, cutting her off as she looked down her nose at her. "I'm not an idiot."

Julia pulled Jessie into her side for a quick hug. The teenager wriggled away, dark strands of her hair slipping out of her hood.

Julia was about to ask if Dot was still waiting outside, but she heard a soft sniffle float in her direction. She looked at Jessie, who seemed to have heard it too.

"Wait here," Julia ordered.

"Fat chance," Jessie said, sticking to Julia's side. "You jump, I jump."

"Isn't that a line from *Titanic*?"

"Your DVD collection sucks," Jessie said, her cheeks flushing. "It's infecting my brain!"

They walked out of the sitting room side by side. Julia looked around the entrance hall, but she could not see where the sniffle had come from. Just when she was about to give up hope, she heard it again.

"It came from that door," Jessie said, nodding to a white door concealed in the side of the staircase. "What's in there?"

"No idea," Julia said with a shrug, never having noticed the door before. "Shall we find out?"

They walked slowly towards the door, another sniffle drifting from underneath. Julia wrapped her hand around the cold brass doorknob, twisting it carefully.

She pulled on the door, light pouring down a concrete set of stairs leading to what she assumed was the basement. The smell of must and damp drifted up, along with an ice-cold draft.

"*Hello?*" Julia called into the dark, her voice bouncing off the walls and back at her.

There was a rustle of paper and another sniffle.

Julia headed down the stairs, the freezing air gave her goosebumps. She reached the bottom with Jessie hot on her heels. A single light bulb hung from the low ceiling. It illuminated Dawn, who was resting against one of the stone walls, her hands behind her back, tears streaked down her face.

"It's freezing," Jessie whispered, her hot breath turning to condensation in the air. "What are you doing down here, lady?"

"I needed a minute on my own," she whispered back, paper rustling behind her back. "It's been a rough night."

Dawn stared into Julia's eyes, the single light bringing out the red in her strawberry blonde hair. Instead of being fashionably straight like when Julia had first met her, it was frizzy and draped across her face. Her bright pink nose twitched as she sniffled, tears streaming down her face. Julia found it odd that she was not even attempting to wipe them away.

"She's hiding something," Jessie said, pointing at the grieving mother. "What've you got there?"

"It's nothing," she said, shaking her head, clearly scared of Jessie. "Honestly, it's nothing."

"If it's nothing, show us," Jessie demanded, jumping forward with her hand out. "C'mon. I'm turning into an ice cube down here!"

Dawn pushed herself into the wall even more, her head shaking. She looked past Jessie to give Julia an imploring look. Before Julia could do anything, Jessie launched herself at Dawn.

"*Jessie!*" Julia cried, watching in disbelief as Jessie performed an impressive restraint on the woman's shoulders, making her drop the paper in a heartbeat. "Get off her!"

Jessie scrambled to pick up her prize. When it was in her hands, she ran across the basement, squinting into the dark.

"'*To Dawn*,'" she read aloud. "'*I'm so sorry to do this to you. After reading this, you'll understand. I hope you don't hate me too much, it's just —*'"

Dawn shoved Jessie and snatched the letter back, ripping it clean in two. Jessie held her torn half away from Dawn, but Julia had seen enough. She grabbed the piece of paper from Jessie and passed it back to Dawn, who immediately backed away towards the staircase, her face twisted in disgust.

"I'm sorry," Julia said. "Jessie is just —"

"What's *wrong* with you people?" Dawn cried, stumbling backwards up the first step. "You're *animals!*"

With her torn letter in her hands, she turned and ran back up to the house, tripping every couple of steps.

"Jessie," Julia said, crossing her arms. "There are *better* ways to uncover secrets than *attacking* people."

"I didn't attack," Jessie muttered, looking down at her shoes. "She could have been holding a knife. It was self-defence."

"A knife made of paper?" Julia asked, arching a brow. "Where did you learn that shoulder trick, anyway?"

"Billy taught me."

Jessie's expression suddenly dropped, as though she had just remembered about Billy for the first time since entering the manor. Julia wrapped her arm around Jessie's shoulder, and they walked up the stairs side by side.

Frozen to the core, Julia was glad to close the basement door. Jessie shrugged her arm off before pulling out her phone. She stared blankly at the screen, which had a picture of her and Billy as the background, the countryside behind them. They were both grinning from ear to ear, their cheeks pushed together.

"I took this the day before he told me about the army," Jessie said. "We walked out to Burford and had a picnic. It was freezing, but I didn't care."

To Julia's surprise, Jessie began to sob. She did

not try to hold her tears in, nor did she try to wipe them away. Instead, she pushed her face into Julia's shoulder and tucked her hands tightly around Julia's waist. Nine months down the line, this was a first for Julia.

"It'll get easier," Julia whispered, stroking Jessie's hair as she fought back her own tears. "I promise."

"I don't *want* it to get easier," she sobbed. "I don't want him to go."

Julia had no idea how to reply. She had seen many of Jessie's moods, from her lows to her highs, but she was not sure she had ever seen her so vulnerable and honest. Knowing nothing she could say would make a difference, Julia hugged tighter, resting her head on Jessie's hood.

When she finally pulled away, Julia let her go into the downstairs bathroom alone to clean up. She wandered down the hall to the arch leading into the sitting room, jumping back a step when she saw the back of Ethan's head, his lips pressed against Dawn's as they clung to each other on the ornate red and gold couch.

"I promise, it'll get easier," Ethan said after pulling away and hooking his finger under his wife's chin. "I should know."

Julia crept back carefully, not wanting to intrude on the private moment. She waited by the downstairs bathroom, listening as Jessie forcefully blew her nose. The study door opened, catching her attention. Barker stepped out, followed by who she at first thought was Theo, until she saw the nose bending to the left of his face.

Julia's heart dropped to the pit of her stomach when she realised she had not just seen Ethan kissing his wife, but Theo kissing his sister-in-law. Her eyelids flickered, but all she could do was smile weakly ahead at Barker and his brother as they hugged by the study door.

"*Jessie*," Julia whispered out of the corner of her mouth, knocking on the door. "*Hurry up.*"

***

WHEN SHE WAS SATISFIED THE UPSTAIRS bathroom was empty, Julia pulled Jessie inside and locked the door behind them. She walked over to the freestanding bath in the middle of the large, elegant room, her mind whirring.

"This is where they pee?" Jessie said, looking around the huge space. "It's bigger than my bedroom!"

"I saw Theo kissing Dawn," Julia blurted out, unable to contain it. "Not Ethan. *Theo.*"

"Okay?"

"Dawn is *Ethan's* wife," Julia said. "I thought I saw Ethan kissing Dawn, but then I realised it was Theo."

"But they're twins," Jessie said, crossing her arms and frowning at Julia like she had lost the plot. "How can you tell them apart? They looked pretty identical to me, and you *do* need your eyes testing."

"Who did you say Barker was interviewing when I first woke up?"

"Ethan."

"I saw Ethan coming out of the study while Theo was in the sitting room kissing Dawn," Julia explained. "Ethan has a crooked nose, Theo doesn't."

Jessie looked like she was about to ask another question, but her eyes suddenly widened, and her jaw dropped as her focus drifted past Julia to the window. Julia turned to see what had caught her attention, her stomach turning when she spotted it.

"*Gran?*" Julia cried as she stared into the eyes of Dot, who was inexplicably hovering in front of the window, the blanket tied around her neck like a cape. "What on *Earth* are you doing?"

"She's a *witch*!" Jessie cried. "I *knew* it!"

"Can you let me in?" Dot's muffled voice called through the closed window, her breath steaming up the glass. "It's cold."

Julia yanked on the stiff frame, tugging it up far enough for Dot to crawl through. Metal clattered under her feet as she squeezed through the gap with Julia and Jessie's assistance. When she was firmly inside, Julia peered out of the window and stared disbelievingly down at the tall ladder leaning against the manor.

"Found it in the shed," Dot announced proudly as she straightened out her tight curls in the mirror. "Told one of the officers I saw someone in the woods, and the boy was silly enough to believe me."

"What are you doing here?" Julia whispered as she dragged down the window. "You're not allowed."

"Jessie is!" Dot cried, looking at the teenager in the reflection of the mirror. "If *she* is, *I* am. I was beginning to think the strangler had taken her, so obviously, as her sort-of grandmother, I *had* to come looking for her."

"And you couldn't use the door?" Jessie asked with a smirk. "Like I did?"

"Barker and his brother were in the kitchen. I

knew he would tell me to go away, so I thought on my feet."

"And climbed an unsecured ladder in the pitch-black up to a window you didn't even know was unlocked?" Julia said, somehow not even slightly surprised. "I'm not going to say another word."

"I saw the light turn on when I was carrying the ladder across the garden," Dot said. "It was either the bathroom, or your father's bedroom, and I would have rather taken my chances scaring someone on the toilet than having to listen to Katie squawk and squeak at me."

When she was satisfied with her hair, Dot pulled herself away from the mirror, untied the blanket, and perched on the edge of the bathtub. She crossed her legs, rested her hands on her lap, and stared expectantly at Julia.

"*So*?" she cried. "Fill me in! Who are the suspects? What have you uncovered? I assume the killer is still lurking the halls because I haven't seen anyone leave yet, aside from you and Barker on your little walk."

"I thought you were asleep?"

"I *wanted* you to think I was asleep," Dot said, winking playfully. "First rule of surveillance is to always keep everyone on their toes. I knew you'd try and convince me to go if you thought I was awake, and I was providing a *very* useful service out there. The killer could have fled at any moment!"

"Well, maybe you should get back to that," Julia said, putting her arm around Dot and leading her to the door. "Because you can't stay."

"*Julia South*!" Dot cried, pulling away and resuming her place on the edge of the bathtub. "I am your *grandmother*! I *demand* to know what is going on. My mind has been whirring out there. The silence isn't fun."

"It's better than word association," Jessie muttered under her breath as she climbed into the large bathtub behind Dot. "You might as well fill her in, Julia. She might be able to figure it out."

"Exactly," Dot said with a stern nod as she turned back to Jessie. "That's the smartest thing you've ever said."

"I say smart things all the time," Jessie fired back, her eyes narrowing on Dot. "You're just never there to hear them."

"I'm sure," Dot said with a strained smile as she turned back to Julia. "Suspects?"

Julia exhaled heavily, realising she had nothing to lose. It was not like she had it all figured out on her own.

"First, we have Casper and Heather." Julia began to pace across the black and white tiles. "I think they gave some money to Luke, but I'm not sure why or how much. It's connected to his job making apps."

"Making what?" Dot asked, her head recoiling.

"Apps," Jessie said.

"What's apps?" Dot asked, turning to Jessie. "Is it some kind of new drug?"

"They're in phones," Julia explained. "Think games and social media."

Dot blinked heavily, still none the wiser. Julia shook her head to let her gran know it was not an important detail in the story.

"Then there's Conrad and Bella," Julia continued. "Bella is Theo's daughter. Theo is Barker's brother and is also Ethan's twin brother. We'll come to him later."

"Conrad was having it off with Luke," Jessie jumped in. "Luke's the guy who was strangled."

"Conrad is Bella's boyfriend," Julia said, halting her pacing to make sure her gran was following. "They're famous on the internet. That part, I don't understand either."

"Says he's got one hundred and ninety-eight thousand followers here," Jessie said after tapping on her phone. "Look."

Julia squinted at the number, which was above a line with an email for businesses to contact him regarding '*engaging sponsored content*'. Below that, Julia could see three pictures. The first was a picture of Conrad wearing nothing but tight, black underwear, standing in the middle of a nicely decorated apartment. The second was a picture of Conrad and Bella kissing, Peridale Manor behind them. Bella was wearing the same clothes she had on when asking for directions in Julia's café. The last picture was a blurry shot, but Julia could not make it out. She looked at Jessie for an explanation, who consulted the phone, tapped the picture, quickly turning it into a video.

"Something *awful* has happened," Conrad said, tears in his eyes, a black and white filter over the video. "Someone close to us has been *murdered*, and the police are keeping us *hostage* at Peridale Manor. Spread the word. I *finally* understand what police brutality feels like!"

Conrad then turned to Bella, who had been sobbing in the background the whole time. The video ended and looped back to the beginning, forcing Jessie to tap off it and back to the layout of the pictures and follower numbers.

"Ugh," Jessie cried. "What *awful* people."

"Police brutality?" Julia echoed through an unimpressed laugh. "What does that even mean?"

"I don't know," Jessie said, scrolling down on her phone. "The top comment says *#FirstWorldProblems* and the next one says *#YourWhitePrivilegeIsShowing*. Some people are taking it seriously though. *#SaveConradandBella*. Fifty-two *thousand* people have viewed the video. That's impressive."

"Well, he seems like a twerp," Dot said with a final nod. "And they looked like they were hiding in a cupboard. So, he's the one who was having it away with the victim, but that's his girlfriend?"

"Yes," Julia said, impressed that Dot was keeping up. "Then we have Dawn, Ethan, and Theo. I just saw Theo and Dawn kissing."

"But you said they were twins," Dot said, her eyes crinkling at the sides. "How could you tell?"

"One has a crooked nose," Jessie announced. "One doesn't."

Dot tapped her finger on her chin for a moment as she absorbed the information.

"Money and revenge," she said after a moment of silence. "The only reasons to kill someone. It was either the uncle and aunt, or the crying video couple."

"*Or* Luke knew something about the affair," Jessie added. "Maybe they were trying to silence him. I *acquired* a letter written to Dawn. It seemed like an apology or something. I only read the first few lines."

"Or it's something else entirely," Dot suggested, her finger tapping harder. "Do you have any clues?"

Julia pulled her phone out of her pocket and flicked to the picture of the mystery fleshy blur.

"Why do you have a bottom on your phone, Julia?" Dot asked as she held the phone at arm's length, her head tilting. "How *rude*!"

"Told you," Jessie said. "Butt cheek."

Dot swiped her finger dramatically across the picture and landed on the picture of the footprints on the carpet Julia had taken.

"This person has one foot," Dot said, tilting her head even more.

"*What*?" Julia took her phone back and examined the picture she had yet to look at. "How can you tell?"

Dot snatched the phone back and double-tapped on the screen, something she must have seen someone else do because she did not own a mobile phone.

"*One foot*," she said again, her voice rising.

"What is that? Paint?"

"Lotion," Julia corrected, sitting next to her gran and leaning into the picture. "Oh, wow. You're right. I hadn't given that picture much thought."

"Why aren't you concerned that a one-footed man is walking around the place?" Dot cried, passing the phone back. "That's like something out of a horror movie!"

"Because I know who the one foot belongs to," Julia said, tapping the phone against her chin. "And he failed to mention that he'd visited his nephew's bedroom."

CHAPTER 9

Julia opened the bathroom door, surprised when she came face to face with Hilary. The housekeeper was wearing a white nightie; her surprisingly long hair flowed freely across her shoulders, and her eyes were free of the usual liner. From the look on her face, she was just as surprised to see Julia.

"Oh," she grunted, looking past Julia to Dot

and Jessie. "I won't ask."

"We were discussing suspects," Dot exclaimed before shoving past the housekeeper. "Nice nightie."

Hilary pursed her lips as she stared down at Dot, somehow looking less menacing without her usual prim and proper exterior; she almost looked human.

"We'll get out of your way," Julia said, looking at the door to Casper and Heather's room over Hilary's shoulder.

Julia and Jessie shuffled past the housekeeper, who walked into the bathroom after them. Instead of closing the door, she headed straight for the medicine cabinet to search through the bottles. A frustrated sigh let Julia know she could not find what she was looking for.

"Lost something?" Julia called back into the bathroom as she leaned against the doorframe.

"It's nothing," she said with a dismissive wave of her hand. "It's just – I seem to have *misplaced* my blood pressure pills. I must have put them down somewhere, but I can't remember where. I could have *sworn* they were on my bedside table."

"Old age can do that to you," Dot said with a knowing nod, despite having at least fifteen years on Hilary. "They'll turn up where you least expect them. Have you checked the fridge? I once found my slippers in there. To this day I still have no idea how they got there."

"I'll find them," Hilary snapped. "I haven't lost them, I just don't know where they are right now."

"Need some help?" Julia offered, eager to return the favour after Hilary's tip-off over the cookies. "Four sets of eyes are better than one."

"I said, I'll find them."

Hilary pushed past Julia and shuffled across the hallway towards her bedroom, pausing to glance over the bannister at DS Christie as he chatted to the officer on the door.

"Maybe she wouldn't need blood pressure pills if she wasn't so *tightly* wound," Dot exclaimed, her lids fluttering as she pushed up her curls. "I've *always* been a very *relaxed* person, and my blood pressure has always been *impeccable*."

"*Relaxed*?" Jessie scoffed with a roll of her eyes. "And I'm the Queen of England."

"*Shush!*" Dot whispered, mushing her finger against Jessie's lips. "Did you hear that?"

"Hear what?" Jessie muffled through the finger, her eyes narrowed.

Julia listened in the direction Dot's ear was pointed, but she could not hear anything.

Dot released Jessie's lips before hurrying down

the hallway, stopping at the last door on the other side of Katie's great-grandfather's bust. Dot sprung open the door, and to Julia's surprise, Conrad and Bella were squashed up on the floor underneath the boiler.

"*Hey!*" Conrad cried, squinting into the light. "We have *rights!*"

"Why are you hiding in the airing cupboard?" Dot asked, planting her hands on her hips. "You look ridiculous!"

"We *refuse* to take part in this investigation!" Bella cried, wriggling in the tight space, her legs clearly hurting. "We're letting the world know about this. It's *illegal* to keep us here! We've researched it."

"I *really* hate them," Jessie whispered to Julia as they stood behind Dot. "*Please,* can I punch one of them?"

"Threats of *violence!*" Conrad cried, pulling out his phone with shaky hands. "Do you want to say that again for my one hundred thousand followers?"

Dot snatched the phone from the boy and tossed it down the hallway. It vaulted along the floorboards before bouncing down the stairs, rattling and cracking as it hit each marble step.

"*That's my property!*" he cried, his voice squeaking, reminding Julia of Katie. "I'll have you *arrested* for that!"

"Which one do you want to speak to, Julia?" Dot asked, ignoring the handsome young man as his orange streaked face turned a violent shade of red. "Innocent people don't hide in cupboards."

"You *can't* make us leave," Bella said, a little more unsurely. "We have *rights!*"

Julia wondered how she could explain that Dot cared about their rights to hide in a cupboard as much as she cared about the expensive mobile phone she had just flung down the stairs. From the terrified look on Bella's face, it was obvious Dot was somehow conveying that with her tight expression.

"C'mon, Becky," Dot said as she leaned into the cupboard to grab the girl's arm. "Time to stretch your legs."

"It's *Bella!*"

From the horrified look on Barker's niece's face as Dot pulled her out of the cupboard and dragged her towards the bathroom, it was obvious it had been a long time since anyone had ignored her. Julia wondered if it had something to do with the eleven thousand strangers backing her up online.

"In you go," Dot said, pushing Bella into the bathroom with the strength of a woman a quarter her age. "You might want to use the quiet time to reflect on your life choices."

Bella stumbled into the bathroom, her brown and blonde hair cast dramatically across her alarmed face. Before she could say a word, Dot shut the door.

"Jessie, hold this in place," Dot said, clinging to the doorknob as Bella rattled it on the other side. "Becky will tire out eventually."

"It's *Bella*!" she cried through the wood. "*Bella*!"

Jessie took over holding the handle, leaving Dot to march back to the cupboard. She stood over Conrad, and without needing to say a word, he scrambled to his feet. Julia was too impressed to berate her grandmother for her ham-fisted tactics. If they had not worked so effectively, she might have interjected.

"I need a cup of tea," Dot said with a wave of her hand. "I can only handle stupid in small doses."

As though shrinking back to the little old lady she was, Dot slowly made her way down the long staircase. She cast an eye over the shattered phone at the bottom before wandering into the kitchen.

"I – I -" Conrad blurted out. "She'll *pay* for that!"

"Why don't we get some fresh air?" Julia suggested, smiling as politely as she could. "You look like you need it."

BIRTHDAY CAKE AND BODIES

***

"GET YOURSELF A CUP OF TEA," JULIA SAID to the young officer guarding the front door. "You look like you need a break."

"Are you sure?" he asked with a relieved smile. "It's been a long night."

"You look frozen through, and the kitchen is nice and warm. I'll keep watch for fifteen minutes."

The officer let out a thankful sigh before heading into the house. Julia walked into the icy night and sat on the cold stone doorstep, patting the space next to her for Conrad to follow.

"Are you some kind of police officer?" he asked as he perched stiffly next to her. "I thought you worked in a café?"

"I do," Julia said as she looked up at the bright half-moon peeking out from behind the faint clouds. "I'm helping on an unofficial basis."

"That means I don't have to tell you anything," he said defiantly, relief spreading across his smug face. "I know my -"

"Rights?" Julia jumped in. "You're correct, you don't have to tell me anything, but when you hear what I have to say, I think you might want to explain yourself."

Conrad narrowed his sparkling blue eyes on her, his blond hair glowing in the dark. Despite his streaky fake tan, his thick hair looked natural. She could see how he had gained so many followers online based on his looks.

"I know you visited Luke's bedroom right before he was murdered," Julia started. "And I know you spent twenty-five minutes in his room."

It became obvious from the way Conrad's eyes sprung open he had thought his visit was still his little secret.

"*I – He –*" Conrad stuttered, his cheeks darkening. "We were discussing business. He was developing a new app, and he wanted me to promote it."

"I don't doubt that," Julia said confidently. "Do you usually conduct your business meetings naked?"

Conrad's eyes widened even more. His lips parted, but all he could do was gasp like a fish out of water; he knew he had been caught out.

"I'm not judging you," Julia said. "Well, maybe I'm judging that you're in a relationship with his cousin."

"It's my *brand*."

"Brand?"

"I can't be gay," he said with a heavy sigh as he

planted his face in his hands. "Big parts of my audience are heterosexual men. Not all, but a lot of them won't buy protein powder and food supplements from a gay guy, no matter how much I work out."

"That's not very fair."

"But it's *true*," he said, turning to Julia, the seriousness in his face making her believe him. "You have *no* idea how cut-throat it can be when it comes to building an online persona that can get brand deals. When I started posting pictures with Bella, my engagement went up overnight. Companies started paying me more. It all just slotted into place. I became '*aspirational*'. Guys see the pretty girlfriend and the good body, and they want to buy whatever I'm talking about so they can be like me."

"But it's fake."

"*So?*" Conrad laughed, shaking his head. "*Nothing* online is *real*. It's all filtered and processed. We frame our lives to make them look perfect. Even if we're not making money from it, we *never* post the bad pictures. People see an image of my six-pack, and they think I rolled out of bed looking like that. They don't see that I don't drink water the day before the photo-shoot so I don't bloat up, and that I'm exhausted from the three hundred sit-ups I've just done. I breathe in, take twenty pictures, and then I pick the one that looks the best. It's not easy, but it's just the way things are. You *must* understand."

"I only really post pictures of my cakes," Julia admitted. "I'm not really into the online thing."

"But I bet you don't post the pictures that make your cakes look bad, do you?"

"Well, of course not, but -"

"It's *no* different," he jumped in. "*I'm* the cake. *I'm* the product. *I'm* selling *me*. Bella helps me sell it. She's part of the image."

"Does she know you're using her?"

Conrad suddenly turned away from Julia. He dropped and shook his head.

"I *know* it's wrong," he said glumly. "But she's benefitting from it too. She has gone from three to eleven thousand in the four months we've been together. *Four months.* It's not easy to grow that quickly without someone with more followers helping. It's a two-way street. When she gets to fifty thousand, she can start selling, and then she's got a job."

Julia knew she was never going to understand the warped logic behind it. She could not imagine living her life for the sake of selling a lie, so she decided to change the course of her questioning.

"How did you meet Luke?"

"In London," he started, before inhaling the cool night air as he looked up at the moon. "I was meeting with a sportswear brand for a business lunch. He was at the bar after his own meeting. He recognised me from Bella's pictures. We had only been together for a week at that point, but she'd been posting since our first date. We started talking. I liked him. I didn't even know he liked me in *that* way, but I was staying in London that night, and he took me to Heaven."

"Heaven?"

"It's a gay club," he explained. "It's quite famous. I'm surprised you haven't heard of it."

"I'm not the club type," Julia explained with an apologetic smile. "Haven't set foot in one since my twenties."

"We had some drinks, and one thing led to another," he continued. "I *really* liked him, and he promised to help my career. We saw each other every chance we got. He lived in London, and I was constantly getting the train in for meetings, so it was easy. I hadn't seen him for three weeks until coming here. I'd missed him *so* much. When he went for that nap, I knew it was code for me to follow. I *thought* I was being careful. I could have sworn nobody saw me. I don't care what you think because I didn't *kill* him. I was falling in *love* with him."

"I believe you," Julia said, his honesty refreshing. "But someone did, and that's what I need to figure out. You probably knew him better than his own family. Did he tell you anything about them?"

"Not really," Conrad admitted with a shake of his head. "I only really know Bella and Theo. I'd never met the others until I came here."

"So, there's nothing he told you?"

"There was the money."

"What money?"

"He was in debt," Conrad said, his eyes narrowing as he stared at the gravel. "A *lot* of debt. About three hundred thousand pounds. It's not like he didn't have money coming in. His company was a big deal, but business is complicated. He said he was stressed about paying the money back because the bank was putting pressure on him."

"Did he say what bank?" Julia asked, pulling her notepad from her pocket along with a small pencil. "That might be helpful."

"He didn't," Conrad said with a shake of his head. "He didn't even say it was a bank, but where else do you get money from these days?"

Julia snapped her notepad shut, knowing exactly where Luke could have got the money.

"You've been very helpful," Julia said, pushing her notepad back into her jeans pocket without needing to make any notes. "Thank you."

"Oh, is that it?" Conrad asked as they both stood up. "You're not going to arrest me?"

"Having a love affair isn't a crime in this country," Julia said with a soft smile. "Although, I suggest you think about if the money you're gaining from Bella's image is worth your integrity."

Conrad nodded, giving off the impression it was something that had been weighing on his mind for months. Julia suspected she was the first person who had been so blunt when it came to his '*job*'.

Julia walked back into the entrance hall as the officer walked out of the kitchen with a steaming cup of tea clasped in his hands.

"Your gran made a pot," he explained before taking a sip. "She's really sweet."

"*Sweet*?" Conrad scoffed. "Are you sure you're talking about the same –"

Darkness abruptly fell on the entrance hall, cutting Conrad off mid-sentence. She felt the young model edge closer to her side.

"*Power cut!*" Dot exclaimed as she shuffled out

of the kitchen with a teapot in her hand. "Typical!"

"*Theo*!" a shrill voice came from the sitting room. "*Stop it*!"

Julia and the officer wasted no time running to the archway. With only the moonlight casting a silvery glow on them, Theo and Ethan were scrambling together on the floor, Dawn and Barker attempting to pull them apart.

"What's going on?" Julia cried, noticing that Theo had Ethan's shirt in his fists. "*Stop it*!"

Dawn pulled Theo off his twin brother with a forceful tug and stood between them, her hands on Theo's chest. Barker pulled Ethan's arms behind his back, his face bright red as he fought to release himself like a savage animal.

"Do I need to arrest you?" Barker cried at his twin brothers. "This *needs* to stop!"

Theo dropped his head, his body convulsing as he laughed frostily to himself. Silence fell on the tense room as the pressure bubbled up. Theo pushed Dawn to the side and launched forward, his fist primed. Theo aimed to punch Ethan, who ducked out of the way, leaving Barker's nose to absorb the force of Theo's knuckles.

"*Barker*!" Julia cried out, rushing to his side in the middle of the battle zone.

BIRTHDAY CAKE AND BODIES

Theo stumbled back as he stared down at his split knuckles. He blinked heavily as though he had just awoken from a nightmare. Julia looked up at Barker, his eyes wide with rage as he clung to his bleeding nose.

CHAPTER 10

"*O uch!*" Theo winced as Julia dabbed the cold cloth against the cuts. "This really isn't necessary."

"Do you want to get an infection?" Julia soaked up the rest of the blood before holding his hand up to the kitchen window. "I don't think it needs stitches."

"I still think I should arrest him, boss," DS

Christie snapped from his position at the door. "He assaulted an officer."

"It's fine," Barker said again for the third time, his voice muffled as Dot worked on applying butterfly stitches to the split across the bridge of his nose. "He's my brother."

"I wasn't aiming for you," Theo said with a small shrug. "I'm sorry, bro. You know I would never hit you on purpose."

"You shouldn't be hitting anyone," Julia said before grabbing the antiseptic spray from the first-aid box. "This will hurt."

He winced as she covered the red cuts in the spray. When she was satisfied they were clean, she applied a wad of dressing before wrapping it up in a bandage. She secured it in place with a piece of bandage tape before finally letting go of his hand.

"You'll live," she said as she patted him on the shoulder. "Just don't do it again."

"Thank you," he replied, opening and closing his fingers. "It's been a weird night."

"*Candles!*" Katie announced shrilly as she wobbled into the room clutching two already lit candlesticks. "Brian is down in the basement looking at the fuse box. I've been telling him we need to replace it for months, but do men ever listen?"

Katie placed one of the candles on the kitchen island and the other on the counter near the patio doors, prime positions to wash the kitchen in their yellow glow.

"You're done," Dot said, dusting off her hands as she stepped back to assess her handiwork. "Gives you an edge."

"Thanks," Barker said with a subdued smile as he slid off the stool. "Hopefully those painkillers will kick in soon."

"They're the good ones," Katie said with a wink. "You'll be on cloud nine within the hour."

Clutching her lower back, Katie shuffled out of the room, followed quickly by Dot.

"No hard feelings?" Theo asked Barker, his hand outstretched.

"Sure." Barker slapped his hand into Theo's. "Just promise me you'll stay away from Ethan."

"Okay."

"That's not the same as a promise, boss," DS Christie jumped in. "I still think you should nick him."

Barker slapped DS Christie on the shoulder as he walked through to the entrance hall. DS Christie looked Theo up and down before doubling back to follow Barker back into the study.

"What a mess," Theo said, leaning against the island. "I should never have come here. I work for the St. John's Ambulance and had to take this as sick days because I had no holidays left."

"We weren't to know this would happen," Julia said, rubbing his back softly. "I just wanted to throw Barker a nice party. I never knew things were so tense, especially since –"

"The funeral?" Theo jumped in, smiling softly at Julia in the glow of the flickering candle. "A similar thing happened on that day. I swore I'd never look my twin brother in the eyes again, but something compelled me to come."

Julia pulled her hand away when she remembered Theo and Dawn's kiss in the sitting room. Perhaps like Conrad, Theo had followed his heart to the manor?

"Family can be tricky," Julia said as she walked over to the oven. "The gas should still be working. How about a nice cup of peppermint and liquorice tea?"

After filling and boiling a pan, Julia grabbed two teabags from the cupboard. She placed the cups on the edge of the island and pulled the candle towards the stools. She sat down and picked up the tea, the sweet and familiar scent soothing her.

"Unusual," Theo said after slurping the hot tea. "I like it."

"It's an acquired taste."

"I suppose you want to know why I felt compelled to hit Ethan?" Theo suddenly asked, his tongue running over his moist lips. "I've seen you running around the place asking everyone questions. Barker has you well trained."

Julia pursed her lips, resenting the idea that she was nothing more than Barker's lap dog. She wanted to mention the half a dozen times she had outwitted Barker by solving a murder case before him, but she bit her tongue, deciding it would bring nothing to the table other than a sour feeling.

"It did cross my mind," she said airily. "It's not my place to ask personal questions, is it?"

"He thinks his grief was worse than mine," Theo said with a cold laugh. "He genuinely believes his son being strangled is worse than what happened to my Bethany."

"He said that?"

"His exact words were '*you'll never understand what this feels like*'," Theo said with another cold laugh. "If only he knew what I knew."

"Slip of the tongue?"

"From Ethan?" Theo snapped. "He's always

been calculated and cold. He ruined my life getting into that car with Bethany. He deserves everything he gets."

Julia sipped her hot tea, Theo's sobs in the bathroom echoing around her mind. Had he been crying for the memory of Bethany, rather than his murdered nephew?

"It's been a long day," Julia said. "I'm sure you can talk in the morning. Tempers are running high."

"Talk?"

"You're still brothers."

"We might share a face, Julia, but that man is *not* my brother," Theo said as he slid off the stool. "Thanks for the tea."

Without another word, Theo headed for the door, his bandaged hand running over his bald head. He disappeared into the dark, leaving Julia alone in the flickering candlelight. Trying to remember she was in a house full of people and not alone, she lifted her comforting tea to her lips, blowing at the steam.

"Julia?" a voice hissed in the dark.

Julia dropped the cup, the ceramic shattering on contact with the marble. Hot tea splashed against her blouse, soaking through in seconds. She jumped back with a gasp as she looked up at the doorway. Jessie smiled her apologies from under her hood.

"It's fine," Julia said quickly, pulling the blouse away from her chest as she ripped a paper towel from the roll on the counter. "Has something happened?"

"Bella knows," Jessie whispered, glancing over her shoulder as she stepped into the candlelight. "She knows what Conrad was doing with her cousin."

"Are you sure?"

"She just admitted it," Jessie said, creeping forward before picking up the other cup of peppermint and liquorice tea. "This for me?" Jessie picked up the cup and slurped from the rim before Julia could answer. "When you went to talk to Conrad, I held the door for as long as I could, but she wouldn't give up trying to get out. She told me she wouldn't run if I let go, but she did. I threw a shampoo bottle at her, and she fell over. Once I had her in a restraint, we went into the bathroom together, and we started talking. At first, I was trying to understand the point of her online stuff. She's pretty defensive about it, but she said something like '*Conrad is making it worth my time*', which I found weird. The way she said it made it sound like the relationship was fake, so I straight out asked what she would do if he cheated on her. Just from the look on her face, I knew that she knew."

"You're basing this on a look?"

"She confessed everything," Jessie said, a grin spreading behind the cup. "I asked if Luke had a girlfriend, and she quickly said that he was gay. I asked how she knew, and she stumbled and stuttered. Started singing like a canary. Apparently, she's known since the first day Luke and Conrad met. One of her friends saw them kissing in some bar."

"But that was months ago," Julia muttered, frowning into her tea. "Why not just leave him?"

"She figured out he was using her," Jessie said, her grin growing. "But she was using him from the beginning too. She called it '*social climbing*'. She's using his hundred thousand followers to grow her own profile, so she can make money, and then hop onto another guy with a bigger following."

"So, she was just biding her time?" Julia sipped her tea, her head spinning with the new information. "And she doesn't love Conrad?"

"Not even an ounce, by the sounds of it, but she did seem pretty upset that Luke had been lying to her. She said they used to be friends, even after what happened with Bethany."

"Upset enough to kill him?"

"Who knows?" Jessie said with a shrug.

"Stranger things have happened."

"They have," Julia said, her finger tapping rhythmically against her chin. "I still need to speak to Casper and Heather."

"I saw Casper walking down the stairs. I had to overtake because he was too slow. He was mumbling to himself about the buffet."

***

AFTER JESSIE WENT OFF TO FIND DOT, Julia headed to the sitting room with a candlestick in her hand. She walked through the shadowy entrance hall, the crystal chandelier glittering above in the blackness. She passed the basement door, which was slightly open. She almost called down to see if her father was okay, but she heard him curse and drop what sounded like a screwdriver, so she left him to it.

She walked into the sitting room, pleased to see that Katie had dotted candles around the room. She placed hers on a side table and turned to the buffet table, almost missing Casper entirely.

"*Casper?*" Julia called out, startling the man as he stuffed sausage rolls in his mouth, completely bent over the buffet table. "Hungry?"

The silver foil rustled as Casper spun around,

flaky pastry stuck in his moustache. He dropped his cane in the confusion, wobbling on the spot like a ball on a seesaw. Julia hurried over to steady him before he toppled over entirely.

"I think you might have just witnessed me losing my last shred of dignity," he confessed as he dusted the flakes from his moustache. "Sausage roll?"

Casper hobbled over to the cushioned window ledge. He collapsed into the corner with a pained sigh, his eyes closed as the pressure lifted off his leg. Julia pulled off the foil before joining him with the plate.

"Heather wouldn't let me come down," he said. "She's holding me hostage in the bedroom. Thinks you're going to start trying to pin things on us."

"I don't pin things on innocent people," Julia said as Casper plucked a mini sausage roll from the plate. "I'm just trying to figure out the truth."

"Well, at least you know we're innocent," Casper mumbled through the mouthful. "That's a weight lifted."

"I never said that," she replied with a polite smile. "I know that you visited Luke's bedroom sometime before he died."

"*W-What*?" Casper paused to cough on the sausage roll lodged in his throat. "How-"

"I know about the money too," Julia said before plucking out a sausage roll. "Three hundred thousand pounds is a lot to lend to your nephew."

Julia tossed the sausage roll into her mouth, chewing slowly as she watched Casper's cheeks turn a painful shade of burgundy.

"How do you know about that?" Casper said, his nostrils flaring. "I never told anyone, apart from Heather."

"Know about what?" Julia said. "The bedroom visit, or the money?"

"Both."

Julia licked the flakes off her lips before pulling her phone out of her pocket. She brought up the picture, zoomed in on the single white footprints on the dark carpet, and turned it to Casper. He took the phone from her, his eyes crinkling as he squinted at the grainy image.

"I didn't realise they were single footprints at first," Julia admitted. "It's not something that crossed my mind, but my gran's mind works very differently to the rest of us." Julia picked up another sausage roll as she watched Casper's plump, red face drain to blend in with the white wall behind him. "You did tell me you were rather good at using your crutch when you didn't want to wear your prosthetic."

"I *didn't* kill him."

"I never said you did."

"But you're *implying* it," Casper yelled, his face reddening again. "Heather was right about you!"

Julia paused to think about the impression she had given to Heather, and what she could have been right about.

"Casper, I just want to know what you were doing in your nephew's bedroom, and why you didn't tell anyone."

"You think I did it!" Casper cried, tossing the phone back to Julia. "I just went to talk to him. I knew I had to wait until he was alone. I heard him come upstairs."

"How did you know it was Luke?"

"He switched rooms with Ethan and Dawn," Casper explained. "The housekeeper gave Luke a bigger bed, so Dawn made him switch." Casper picked up another sausage roll and placed it into his mouth before continuing. "That's not important. What's important is I *only* went to talk to him about the money. He hadn't been answering my calls. I even tried emailing him, and I don't even use computers. I don't trust them. Heather had to help, not that the brat replied. I know you shouldn't speak ill of the dead, but that boy was rotten to the core. I should never have trusted him!"

"Where did you get three hundred thousand pounds from?" Julia asked, her voice softening. "That's a lot of money."

Casper's eyes darted down. He turned to look through the window and into the pitch black. Julia turned too, noticing his sad expression in the dark reflection.

"We re-mortgaged," he whispered, the words catching in his throat. "We'd almost paid it off, but he pitched his idea so well. He sold us the dream. We thought we'd be able to finally move abroad with the extra money."

"What did he promise you?" Julia asked, resting her hand on Casper's good knee.

"He said he'd turn our investment into a million pounds in six months," Casper said with a disbelieving laugh. "We were the *fools* who believed him. He told us he'd landed on an idea for a game. He said failure was '*impossible*' and that our money was '*guaranteed*'. Heather was against it, but I was the chump who went along with it. The bank would only give us a ten-year mortgage, so we re-mortgaged for two hundred thousand, and I took the rest from my army pension and life savings. There was enough to pay the repayments for a couple of months, but it ran out quicker than we expected. The camper van needed a new engine, and Heather had to spend a month in Spain when her sister broke her hip. Eventually, the money ran out, and I had – I had to –"

Casper broke off as tears began to collect along his lashes.

"I had to sell my medals," he said, swallowing back the tears. "I didn't even get a decent price for them, but I was desperate. When I saw Luke here acting like nothing had happened, I felt sick. I *wanted* to throttle him, believe me, but I didn't actually do it."

"What did you do?"

"I confronted him," Casper continued. "He was already in bed. I asked him when I'd see my money again, and he told me he'd lost it, like he was talking about some spare change. He said that was '*just business*' and investments are never '*one hundred percent secure*'. I signed something when I handed over the money, which he told me was for my protection, but he revealed that the fine print said I was *donating* the money and I would only receive a return on my investment if the project worked. My own nephew ruined my life, and now that he's dead,

I have no chance of ever seeing that money again."

"Surely that's not legal?" Julia responded, her heart pounding on Casper's behalf. "His company will still exist even though he's gone. There *must* be someone you can talk to."

"I can't afford a lawyer," he said, tears trickling down his cheeks and into his moustache. "I don't even know where I'm going to get the next month's money from. The bank is going to take our home from under us, and we'll be out on the street. We've lived there for thirty years!" Casper paused to wipe away his tears with a shaky hand. "You've got to believe me, I didn't kill him. I threatened him, and he jumped out of bed, bold as brass and stark naked. That was the type of person he was. He was so sure of himself that he didn't even care. I stumbled back and fell into the chest of drawers. My stump was killing me, so I had gone in without my fake leg. The bottle of moisturiser fell off, and I must have stepped in it. I hurried back to him on my crutch and loomed over him, and all he could do was smirk at me. It knocked me sick. I turned around and left. That was the last I saw of him. Katie screamed over an hour later."

"So, you went in before Conrad?" Julia asked, almost to herself. "That rules you out of the frame entirely."

"Conrad?"

"Bella's boyfriend," Julia said. "It doesn't matter, but it puts you in the clear, as long as you've told me the truth."

"I *swear* on my good leg that I have told you *everything*." Casper held his hand up. "I stayed in the bedroom with Heather until he was found."

Julia was about to tell Casper that she believed him, but a loud thudding distracted her. She jumped up, the sausage rolls falling off her knee. The tray clattered against the floorboards and sent the nibbles rolling across the floor.

Snatching up the candlestick as she went, Julia hurried back into the entrance hall, her heart stopping when she saw the figure in the white nightie lying at the bottom of the stairs. At that very moment, the lights flickered back on.

"What was *that?*" Brian cried as he ran up the stairs from the basement.

All of the doors at the top of the hallway opened, and Heather, Bella, Conrad, Dawn, Ethan, Theo, and Katie all appeared, each of them looking as astounded as the other when they saw the lifeless body at the bottom of the stairs.

"*Hilary?*" Dot cried when she came from the

dining room with Jessie. "What happened?"

"Someone call an ambulance," Julia said as she crouched by the housekeeper's side, a small pool of blood forming under her wiry hair. "Tell them to be quick."

CHAPTER 11

The paramedics arrived in eight minutes, and four later they were speeding away from Peridale Manor with Hilary strapped to a stretcher, Brian by her side. Five minutes after that, Barker was once again pacing in the sitting room, his family surrounding him.

"Here we are again," Barker said through clenched teeth, his nostrils flared. "Because one body wasn't enough for today."

"She's not dead," Katie reminded him from the window seat where Julia had been sat with Casper and the sausage rolls. She had her mobile phone clutched in her hand, resting on her bump. "They've just arrived at the hospital."

"She could have fallen," Heather suggested quietly, her hand wrapped around Casper's. "Those stairs *are* slippery."

"She's lived here for forty years!" Katie shrieked, her face turning pink. "Hilary could find her way around this house with her eyes closed in the dark. She's never so much as tripped on a carpet."

"I can't believe I'm saying this, but Katie is probably right," Dot said as she fiddled with her brooch. "One of you pushed her."

"I was downstairs with Julia," Casper jumped in, pointing his cane in Julia's direction, who was leaning against the fireplace behind Barker as the dying fire crackled softly against the backs of her legs. "And Heather didn't do it. We were together when Luke died."

"Why are we assuming this is connected?" Theo said as he rubbed his forehead. "As far as we know, Katie or Brian did it."

"I beg your –" Katie jumped up, only stopping

when Julia softly shook her head. "Brian was in the basement, and I was with Daddy."

"Can he verify that?" Bella asked. "Why haven't we seen him?"

"He's in a wheelchair," Julia explained, looking around Barker as he paced in front of her. "He can't talk."

"Next you're going to suggest *he* did it!" Katie cried, both hands clutching her bump. "I need to get out of this room. It's not good for me or the baby."

Julia refrained from blurting out that she thought it was the wisest thing Katie had ever said. She shuffled out in her bright pink slippers and pink silk nightie.

"If she's leaving, then so am I," Dawn said blankly, pushing herself up from the couch. "Come on, Ethan. We don't need to listen to this."

"*Sit down*," Barker demanded. "No one is leaving until we figure this out."

"There's nothing to figure out," Conrad said. "I didn't push her."

"Neither did I," Bella added. "Why *would* I?"

"Why would *anyone*?" Ethan cried as he rolled his head around his neck. "Can we not grieve in peace?"

"Sure," Barker said. "Will the person who

strangled Luke and pushed Hilary please stand up?"

Barker stopped pacing, crossed his arms, and stared out at his family. None of them could look him in the eyes. Casper and Heather clung to each other, as did Bella and Conrad. Ethan and Dawn twitched on either side of the couch they were sharing, and Theo looked down at the ground from his position near the buffet, the only spot in the room where he did not have to make eye contact with his twin brother.

"She must have known something," Jessie spoke up as she traced her finger across the grooves in one of the gold-framed oil paintings hung on the wall. "It's obvious. She must have figured it out and confronted the strangler."

"Makes sense," Dot echoed. "The girl is right. But how did she figure it out?"

"Maybe she knew something we haven't found out yet?" Jessie added, her finger tracing the indentations of a large oak tree. "She must see a lot of stuff."

"Maybe," Julia wondered aloud, suddenly contemplating that Hilary might have held something back during their cookie confessional.

"One of you is keeping a secret," Barker cried, slapping his hands against the side of his head. "*One* of you lied in your interview!"

Julia looked at Theo and Dawn, who were keeping their affair secret, Casper and Heather, who were keeping their money woes secret, and Bella and Conrad, whose entire relationship was a sham. She landed on Ethan, wondering if he was the one Brown who had been honest.

"*None* of you?" Barker cried, looking at each of them. "You've got *nothing* to say? C'mon, guys. I usually can't get a word in edgeways when you're all in the same bloody room!"

A vein in Barker's neck popped out, his breathing deepening as his skin turned purple. Julia rested a hand on his shoulder, hoping it would calm him.

"Boss," DS Christie called from the archway, his phone clenched against his shoulder. "Chief is on the phone. He seems to have the impression we're keeping hostages up here. Dozens of calls have been coming in."

Conrad and Bella's eyes darted down to the coffee table, and they edged in closer to each other.

"*Hostages?*" Barker muttered, his face twisting up. "What hostages?"

"It's *them!*" Jessie cried, pointing at the young couple. "They've been blasting the whole thing on social media. Thousands have seen it!"

"We were scared," Bella mumbled. "We thought you were going to frame us."

"Why would I *frame* you?" Barker cried, his hands on his hips. "Jesus, Bella! You are so stupid sometimes, do you realise that?"

Bella's jaw dropped, as did Dawn's and Heather's. It only took a couple of seconds for Bella to burst into tears and run out of the room. Conrad stood up to leave, but Jessie pushed him back into his seat with a shake of her head.

"Leave her," she said. "I'll go."

It was Dot's turn to drop her jaw. She looked at Julia for an explanation, but all Julia could offer was a shrug. How could she explain that Jessie was turning from a girl into a woman before their very eyes?

"I can't do this anymore," Barker said, staring blankly off into the corner of the room. "I'm done. Kill each other for all I care."

Barker walked out of the room, his heavy head dropped low. Julia wanted to rush after him, but it was Dot's turn to shake her head.

"Leave him," Dot said with a calm smile. "He might say something he regrets. Give the man some space."

Julia forced herself to stay exactly where she was, despite every fibre of her being telling her to run after the man she loved.

"Are *none* of you going to be honest?" she asked, taking Barker's place. "You all know you're lying to him about something."

Once again, all eyes drifted to the floor, including Ethan's. Julia almost pushed it, a big part of her wanting to call out each of them on their deceptions. For the sake of not starting World War Three and stacking up more bodies, she bit hard on her tongue, inhaled calmly, and turned to her gran.

"Can you keep checking in with Dad to see how Hilary is doing?" Julia asked. "I want to know the second she wakes up. She might have seen something."

"*If* she wakes up," Conrad whispered, his eyes vacant and teary. "Why did I come here?"

Just like Bella before him, Conrad ran out of the room in tears.

"Unbelievable," Theo muttered, stepping forward for the first time since entering the room. "The sooner they break up, the better."

Theo followed Conrad out of the room while shaking his head. Heather and Casper also took it as their invitation to flee without being ordered to sit.

The couple hobbled out arm in arm faster than Julia had seen them move before. Ethan also wasted no time leaving his wife's side, his face ghostly pale.

"I think another cup of tea is in order," Dot announced. "Or maybe coffee? I need some matchsticks to hold open my eyes."

Julia turned and looked at the clock on the mantelpiece. She could not believe it was only just approaching two in the morning. She turned back to Dawn, surprised she was the only one not to flee. She attempted to smile at Julia, but her wobbling bottom lip took over; she could not hold back her tears.

Murder investigation or not, Julia was still human. She swooped to Dawn's side, wrapped her arm around her, and pulled the grieving woman against her chest.

"My *son*," she cried, tears flooding from her clenched eyes. "My *only* child."

Julia let Dawn cry until she could not cry anymore. She watched the clock strike two, and then pass it. By quarter past, Dawn could finally sit up straight, tear-streaked and nose runny.

"He was a troubled boy," she choked out as she wiped her nose with her sleeve before tucking her strawberry blonde hair behind her ears. "He was always the same way. Manipulative, even as a child. He could run rings around anyone to get what he wanted. I always told him he would cross someone the wrong way one day, I just never expected it to end up like this."

"Do you have any idea who could have done it?" Julia asked carefully, not wanting to push Dawn over the edge again.

"If I did, you'd have another body on your hands."

Dawn's expression suddenly soured, her eyes turning steely for a brief moment. Julia was wise enough to believe her threat.

"That letter," Julia said, resting a hand on Dawn's knee as her foot tapped impulsively on the floor. "What was it about?"

"It doesn't matter now," Dawn said, looking up at the ceiling as though trying not to cry again. "It has nothing to do with this."

"It might."

"You're suddenly an expert about my family?" she scoffed, turning to Julia with an even sourer expression. "*Who* are you, Julia? You've known Barker for five minutes, and you're trying to push your way into this family when you're not wanted."

"Believe me when I say I'm *not* trying to push

myself into your family," Julia said, her bitter tone matching Dawn's. "From what you've all shown me, I'm sorry I invited any of you to this party."

Julia regretted the words the moment they left her mouth. The dead silence that followed told her Dawn was just as surprised to hear them as Julia had been to say them. Both women joined each other in looking sheepishly down at the floor, as fragile as one another.

"I'm sorry," Dawn said. "I shouldn't have said that."

"Neither should I."

"Shouldn't you?" Dawn forced a dry laugh. "You're right. We *are* a mess. We have been for years. Dysfunctional isn't even the word. I could try and explain everything to you, but we'd still be here long after sunrise."

"Why don't you start with the letter?"

"I told you, it's not connected," Dawn said, her words harsh for a moment before her expression softened. "It's sensitive. I shouldn't be telling you. Nobody knows."

"If it's not connected, I won't breathe a word," Julia promised, resisting the urge to cross her fingers. "You can trust me."

Dawn reached into her pocket, pulling out the

letter. She had taped it back together from when Jessie had ripped it in half. Julia thought she was going to hand it over for her to read, but she clung to it, keeping it closed. The inky pen had bled through the paper, but Julia could not make out any of the backwards words.

"It's a suicide note," she croaked, swallowing hard. "Left by my husband, Ethan."

Julia looked down at the note, and then up at Dawn. She opened her mouth, but no words came out. She shook her head, letting Dawn know she did not understand.

"I found him two weeks ago in our bathroom with a bottle of vodka in one hand and a bottle of pills in the other," she whispered, glancing at the archway. "He'd left this on his pillow in the middle of the night. I usually sleep right through, but I woke up needing the bathroom. I read the note, and I realised what he was going to do, and then I heard him crying. He couldn't go through with it."

Julia thought back to the attractive couple in the designer clothes she had seen step off the train only days previously; it felt like a lifetime ago somehow. She was finding it difficult to comprehend that Ethan would want to do such a thing.

"I never would have known," Julia whispered,

her eyes trained on the letter as her heart pumped. "I'm so sorry."

"How would you?" Dawn asked. "He's good at hiding it. He's always suffered badly with his mental health, but he refuses help at every turn. I've tried over the years, but it's like putting a blanket on someone constantly on fire. It's an illness, we just can't see it. After reading this letter, I almost understand why he went that far. I haven't been able to look at him the same since reading it."

"What does it say?"

Dawn opened the letter and parted her lips as though she was going to read it aloud. She paused, tears welling up in her blue eyes. She snapped the letter shut before handing it carefully over to Julia, who accepted it like a fragile artefact.

"*Julia*?" Dot called from the door. "Your dad called. It's about Hilary."

Dawn immediately snatched the letter back, crammed it in her pocket, and jumped up. She blinked hard at Julia as though she was disgusted she had shared so much. Julia wanted to protest, but Dawn ran out of the room, pushing past Dot as she went.

"How *rude*!" Dot cried as she dusted down her blouse. "Grief is not an excuse to have no manners."

"What is it, Gran?" Julia asked, the disappointment at not reading the letter swelling up inside her. "How's Hilary?"

"She's been rushed into emergency surgery," Dot said, the house phone clutched in her hand. "She's alive, for now, but her skull is cracked. Brian said something about relieving pressure on her brain, and then he got all technical. You know what I'm like with medical mumbo-jumbo. I want to know if it can be cured, or if it'll kill me, and everything else is the stuff in-between."

"So, she's not going to be able to tell us if she was pushed, or if she fell," Julia said, dropping her head into her hands. "I have no idea who did this, Gran. Nothing makes any sense."

"Do you know what you need?"

"What?" Julia asked, looking up hopefully at her gran. "Tell me."

"A nice cup of tea," Dot said, jerking her head for Julia to follow her back into the kitchen. "And I mean a proper cup of strong tea with milk and sugar. None of that peppermint and liquorice modern drivel that you like."

For once, Julia agreed with her gran. She stood up and followed her into the kitchen without another word.

CHAPTER 12

J ulia felt substantially better after her tea break with her gran, who had made sure to chatter about every piece of idle village gossip she could summon rather than rattle on about what was happening around them. She left Dot to wash up in the kitchen, her mind more alert thanks to the caffeine from the tea.

She walked across the marble entrance hall to

her father's study. After knocking softly on the door, she cracked it open, disappointed to see DS Christie alone.

"No Barker?" she asked, disturbing him from his notes.

"He stormed out the front door." He leaned back in his chair, tossing the pen on the table. "I might follow him. I've got the chief breathing down my neck now. Wants an update on what's going on, but what do I tell him? He thinks I should arrest them all one by one and book them until one starts talking, and even then we'd have to drive them out to a station with space."

"You can rule Casper out," Julia offered, closing the door behind her. "And Heather, at least for Luke's murder. They were together in their bedroom when it happened. Casper admitted to visiting Luke, but almost an hour before he was discovered. You'll find out those footprints were his."

"How do you know he didn't just strangle him and leave him there?"

"Aside from the time of death being later in the day, Conrad visited him, remember?"

"Oh, yeah," he said, rubbing his eyes, his brows high up his head. "It's been a long night. Have you confirmed the visit?"

"Conrad confessed everything," Julia said, taking the seat on the other side of the desk, the endless bookshelves lining the room swallowing her up. "Bella knows about the affair too."

"That's a motive at least," he said, picking up his pen again to scribble something down. "Killed her cousin as an act of revenge."

"The affair had been going on for months, and Bella knew from the beginning," Julia said, tilting her head to look at the notes. "It's complicated, but I think you can rule them both out."

"That just leaves Dawn, Theo, and Ethan," he said, sitting up a little straighter and writing a little faster. "Heather and Bella aren't exactly in the clear, but if you have a hunch?"

"I don't think Dawn did it, for what it's worth," Julia said, leaning forward. "Although I have no proof. She's not accounted for during either incident."

"Did you notice that Dawn came out of Theo's bedroom after Hilary was pushed?" DS Christie asked with a dry smirk. "After I realised their noses were different, it was the first thing I noticed. She quickly stepped to Ethan's side, but she came out of his twin's bedroom. Do you think something is going on there?"

"I saw them kissing," Julia offered. "I don't think Conrad and Luke were the only ones having an affair. There's something going on there, but I can't quite put my finger on what."

"Imagine cheating on your husband with his identical brother," DS Christie said, the pen in the corner of his mouth. "I don't see the point."

"They're quite different."

"Yeah," he said with a nod. "Ethan is a bit wet. I know his son's just died, but he needs to man up."

Julia suddenly stood up, everything Dawn had told her heavy on her mind.

"That kind of talk helps no one," Julia said, as calmly as she could. "Just because he's a man, it doesn't mean he has to pretend everything is okay all the time."

"I didn't mean –"

"I know exactly what you meant, DS Christie," Julia said, turning and walking back to the door. "Take it from me, Luke's death isn't the only thing weighing on that man's mind."

"What else is there?"

Julia considered opening up if only to make him regret his comments, but she had promised Dawn she would not mention it to anyone if she did not think it was important to the case.

"It's private," Julia said. "If he wanted you to know, he would have told you in his interview."

Leaving DS Christie to his notes, Julia slipped out of the room. She strode into the middle of the entrance hall, and spun on the spot, wondering where Barker could be. Deciding to take up the detective sergeant's tip-off, Julia slipped past the officer on the front door, who had changed since her meeting with Conrad, and into the freezing air.

The cold hit her like a brick. Every hair on her body rose up, letting her know it was wrong to be out there. She immediately began to shiver, her teeth clattering together loudly, as though she had just jumped into a lake on Christmas Day.

"You might want a coat, miss," the officer said, already taking off his own. "It's a chilly night."

Julia was too cold to protest. She accepted the coat gratefully before stepping off the doorstep onto the gravel. Katie's pink Range Rover and her father's black BMW were parked where they had left them. Two police cars had been parked sloppily behind, and Julia's was where she had skidded to a halt at the opening of the lane. When she saw a shadow moving behind the wheel, she set off towards her little vintage car.

Julia climbed into the passenger seat, not saying

a word to Barker. She rested her head on the headrest, rolled to face him, and smiled. She was warmed even more than by the coat when he returned it.

"I'm sorry," he said, crossing his arms and staring out of the window. "What is it they say about not being able to choose your family? Was I too hard on them?"

"Considering what's happened, no," Julia said. "DS Christie said your boss wants to start arresting them to scare one of them into confessing, and the way things are currently going, I can't say I would blame him."

"Some birthday, huh?"

"I'm sorry."

"This isn't your fault, Julia," Barker reminded her, taking her by surprise by grabbing her cold hand. "You were trying to do something nice, like you always do. You're an amazing woman who got my family together for the first time in three years. Granted, maybe it should have waited another thirty years, but you pulled off the impossible."

"And look how amazing it turned out," she joked, forcing a laugh. "Your birthday cake is still in the boot."

"My chocolate cake?"

"That was a decoy," she admitted. "I made you something more special."

Barker pulled on the door handle and jumped out. He looked into the car as though waiting for Julia to follow him.

"There's cake in the boot," Barker said. "What are you waiting for?"

Julia followed Barker to the back of the car. She popped open the boot expecting the cake to be entirely destroyed, so she was pleasantly surprised to see the cardboard box still in one piece, if not a little battered thanks to her reckless driving on the way there. Julia peeled back the cardboard lid, a smile taking over her face when she saw that the cake was exactly how she had left it.

"The boot acted like a fridge," she murmured as she stared down at the sprinkle covered coconut icing. "I think it's still edible."

Julia thought they might take the cake into the house to cut it up to share amongst the people who wanted a slice, but Barker had other ideas. Using his fist as a shovel, he dug into the cake and scooped up a handful, exposing the bright rainbow layers inside. He wasted no time taking a huge bite.

"*Coconut!*" he exclaimed through the mouthful, sprinkles and icing on his chin and cheeks. "My -"

"Mum's favourite."

"You remembered," he said after swallowing the first piece. "It's really delicious. Try it."

Barker offered his fistful of cake to Julia, who was not too proud to take a bite, especially considering the night she had endured.

"It's good," she said after swallowing. "Pretty perfect, if I do say so myself."

"You've got a little –"

Barker reached out and wiped the tip of Julia's nose, removing a small blob of icing. He licked his thumb with a smile, letting Julia know the Barker she loved was still in there, if not a little buried by Detective Inspector Brown's tough cop routine.

"You've got some too," Julia said, dipping her finger in the cake and wiping it across his cheek. "I think you'll need a napkin for that."

"You too," Barker said, pressing the fistful into the side of her cheek.

Julia stumbled back, her mouth wide open, one eye closed, and half of her face smothered in icing.

"Do you want a war, Barker Brown?" Julia asked, glancing at the massive cake in the boot. "I don't mind wasting my creation on you."

Barker took another bite of the cake, a playful smirk tickling his lips. For a moment, Julia forgot that it was freezing cold, or that they were in the middle of a murder investigation; all that mattered was her, Barker, and the cake.

Julia smeared off the mess on her cheek and readied herself for a full food fight, but a rustling in the bushes behind them froze her. She looked at Barker who seemed to have heard it too. He lifted his finger up to his lips, dropped the fistful of cake, and pulled her behind him. He reached into his pocket and pulled out his phone, swiped up with his thumb, and turned on the flashlight. Like a deer caught in the headlights of a speeding car, a scrawny boy with a cap and a black tracksuit stumbled out of the bushes, the reflective panels down the sides of his clothes shining back at them.

"*Billy?*" Julia asked, squinting through her clear eye. "What are you doing here?"

"The whole village is talking about what's happening up here," he said, his face ghostly white as he shielded his eyes from the bright light. "C'mon, man! It's me."

Barker lowered the light before wiping his hands on the rag Julia kept in her boot for dusting her dashboard. Julia did the same to her hands and face before tucking her hair behind her ears, not caring that one side was now matted with icing.

"There's a road block," he said, looking down the dark winding lane. "I had to come through the fields. There's a whole group gathered down there waiting for something to happen. I heard there were hostages. I couldn't find Jessie, and I wanted to make sure she was okay. She's not answering her phone."

"There are no hostages," Barker said with a roll of his eyes. "What have they put online?"

"There's videos," Billy said, reaching for his phone. "Some girl called Bella has been live streaming on and off all night."

Billy turned the phone around to show them a video of Bella and Conrad curled up on the bed, one of them holding the camera out of reach. There was a loud thud, forcing them both off the bed and towards the door. The live stream cut off, but Julia did not need to see the rest. She noticed that Bella's follower count had risen from eleven thousand to seventeen thousand.

"That definitely rules them both out of pushing Hilary," Julia said, crossing her arms and facing Barker. "That's something."

"I saw an ambulance speeding away from here before," Billy said as he put his phone away, his eyes full of worry. "Please, just tell me about Jessie. Is she okay?"

"She's fine," Julia assured him. "She's in the house."

"Can I see her?"

"Nobody is allowed in," Barker said firmly. "It's a crime scene."

"Barker," Julia whispered softly, looping her hand around his. "Jessie and Dot are there, and we've both been walking around all night. What's one more person?"

Barker pursed his lips down at Julia before nodding somewhat reluctantly at Billy. With Julia and Barker hand in hand, they walked back to the manor with Billy trailing behind, kicking gravel with his trainers as he went.

***

"*B-BILLY?*" JESSIE STUTTERED AS SHE walked out of the downstairs bathroom with Bella, both of them looking like they had been crying. "W-What are you doing here?"

"That's Billy?" Bella asked, rubbing at her red nose with her sleeve. "He's cute."

Barker pushed Billy forward. He stumbled, glancing angrily over his shoulder at them. Julia gave him an encouraging nod. He inhaled deeply, none of his usual teenage bravado anywhere to be seen.

"Hi, Jessie."

"Hi."

"Can we talk?"

"Fine."

Billy followed Jessie back into the downstairs bathroom. The lock clicked in place, sending silence shuddering across the entrance hall.

"Let's leave them to it," Julia said, nodding to the kitchen. "Are you coming, Bella?"

"Oh," she said, caught off-guard by the invitation. "Sure. If you don't mind, Uncle Barker?"

"Of course I don't mind, kiddo."

Julia headed straight for the kettle, but Bella had different ideas. She fished a bottle of white wine from the large clear glass fridge, and three glasses from the cupboard next to it. She filled each glass to the top, making Julia abandon her ideas of peppermint and liquorice tea. She was not much of a drinker, but she did enjoy a glass of white wine every now and then, and this was one of the times she thought she would enjoy it very much.

"Cheers," Bella said, lifting her glass up. "To fresh beginnings. Nothing will ever be the same again."

"I suppose you're right," Barker said, clinking his glass against hers. "I'm sorry about what I said. I didn't mean to call you stupid."

"You were right." Bella took a deep gulp of the wine. "That's why it upset me. Jessie managed to give me some perspective. She's a good kid."

Bella lifted her hand up to her cheek, which had a soft pink mark on it, as though she had recently been slapped very hard.

"I hope she was gentle," Julia said after a soothing sip of the wine, which tasted impossibly more expensive than the bottles she usually picked up from the post office shop. "She's not used to a lot of people her age."

"It was nothing I didn't need," Bella admitted. "I'm ending things with Conrad. She made me realise all of the followers in the world aren't worth the lies."

Barker wrapped his arm around her to give her a reassuring squeeze. She smiled weakly up at her uncle, looking like a little girl. Julia had put her in her early-twenties, but she suddenly looked like a teenager now that she had cried off most of her makeup. She looked old enough to drink, but not old enough to make wise life decisions without a sobering slap across the cheek.

"Maybe I'll join the police," Bella said as she stared into her wine glass. "Follow in my uncle's footsteps."

"Really?" Barker asked, his face lighting up. "It's not for everyone."

"The online life isn't for me," Bella said resolutely. "I was only doing it because everyone else was. I want to really live, ya'know? Experience things. Helping other people might be just what I need."

Just like Julia had with Jessie earlier, she knew she was witnessing the growth of a girl into a woman. She had not liked the '*Bella Belles*' version of Barker's niece very much, but she quite liked the more mature woman sipping wine across the kitchen island.

Julia was about to suggest that Barker give Bella some advice about joining the police force when Dawn ran into the room, a note clutched in her hand.

"Have you seen Ethan?" she cried, tears streaming down her cheeks. "I can't find him, and he's – he's left me *this*."

Dawn handed the note over to Barker, his eyes widening when he saw what was written on it. Bella clasped her hand against her mouth when she read it over her uncle's shoulder. Barker tossed it across the counter to Julia.

She read over it, her heart swelling up into her throat.

"*I'm sorry, Dawn,*" she read aloud. "*I can't live with the guilt. Have a good life. E.*"

CHAPTER 13

"He's not down here," Dot said, casting a finger to the sitting room and dining room.

"And he's not in the bedrooms," Heather added as she propped up Conrad. "Have you checked outside? Maybe he's made a run for it."

"Typical of him to run at the first sign of danger," Theo cried, leaning against the bannister with Dawn sobbing next to him on the bottom step. "Never could stomach confrontation."

"I've got the officers searching the grounds," DS Christie called from the front door. "They didn't see him leave."

"He *could* have crawled out of a window," Dot suggested airily. "Well, the man must be *somewhere!*"

"Search everywhere again," Barker ordered. "Be as thorough as possible. Check every cupboard and small space."

The group reluctantly disbanded, leaving Julia and Dawn alone in the entrance hall. Julia sat next to her at the foot of the stairs, the cold marble stinging her backside.

"He's dead," she whispered, tears streaming down her cheeks. "He's dead, and it's all my fault."

"Where were you when he vanished?" Julia asked, resting her hand on Dawn's shoulder. "And where did you find the note?"

"He left the note on the dressing table in our bedroom, but I was with –"

Her voice broke off, and she began to sob even more. Julia did not need to ask to know exactly whom she was talking about.

"*Theo*," Julia said with a firm nod. "You were with Theo."

Dawn suddenly stopped crying and looked up at Julia, her upset subsiding so confusion could take over.

"H-How did you –"

"I saw you kissing him," Julia explained. "I assumed he was Ethan, until I actually *saw* Ethan. It's the nose."

Dawn began to sob even more, her face clamped in her hands. Julia rubbed her back softly, not wanting the woman to think she was being judged.

"It's complicated," she said when she paused for breath. "You wouldn't understand."

"Try me," Julia said, nodding to the study, which she knew was empty. "Why don't we talk about it in private?"

Dawn nodded as she stumbled up to her feet with Julia's help. Julia almost had to hold the woman up as they walked carefully across the marble floor to the door on the other side. When they were in the study, Julia assumed her father's seat, and Dawn slumped in the chair across from her. With the door closed and the comforting smell of cigar smoke and old books surrounding them, Julia felt happy to be away from the marble perfection of the entrance.

"When did the affair start?"

"It's not an affair," Dawn said, running the back of her hand along her stuffy nose. "Not really. I met Theo before Ethan. It was the summer of 1994. I was taking my niece to see *The Lion King*, and I bumped into Theo and Barker in the lobby. I spilt my popcorn all over him, but he was sweet about it. Theo was nineteen and Barker was fifteen, but they were watching it alone. Everyone was talking about it, so you had to go and see it."

"I remember," Julia said. "I think I was fourteen and my sister was eight."

"After the film ended, Theo slipped me his number," she continued. "I called that night. Peggy answered."

"Peggy?" Julia asked.

"Peggy Brown," Dawn said. "Their mother. She was a formidable woman. She scared me over the phone, but I fell in love with her when I got to know her. She was a baker, just like you, so there was always a cake to try. I loved going there after college. I was taking my A-Levels at the time. Even back then I wanted to be an architect. It's not all it's cracked up to be, but I enjoy it all the same. I can't believe I've been in this beautiful house and not sketched a single thing, but I wasn't expecting any of this.

"We were together up until Christmas. He ended things on December 20th with a phone call. I was heartbroken. He told me he'd met this girl called Michelle. She was blonde and beautiful, and I didn't stand a chance. I had braces and spots back then. I'd met Ethan by that point. I remember him being really into his Sega Mega Drive. I visited the house to give Theo his Christmas present, even though he'd just finished things. I'd bought him a gold chain necklace, and it had cost me months of my weekend job wage.

"Theo wasn't home that night. Nobody was, except for Ethan. He was playing *Sonic the Hedgehog 3*. Peggy had given it to him as an early Christmas present because he hadn't stopped begging for it all year. I wasn't going to stay, but he offered me some pop, and then I just started talking about everything, and I realised how much they really did look alike. Ethan's nose was straight back then. One thing led to another, and before I knew it, I'd switched from Theo to Ethan. I even gave him the gold necklace. I was pregnant with Luke by February 1995. We were still kids ourselves, but it made us grow up quickly.

"I thought I wasn't bothered about any of it. I had my man, and my son, and we got on with things. Theo and Michelle married, and Bethany

197

came the next year. Bella followed two years later. I always wanted a daughter, but it never happened. We tried up until our thirties, but it just wasn't meant to be.

"I'd see Theo at the dinners at Peggy's, and things would be fine. He was civil to me. I convinced Ethan I had never loved Theo and I was just trying to get to him. I don't think he really believed it, but he said he did.

"You have to trust me when I say I never cheated on Ethan. Not once. Not until I came here and I saw Theo for the first time since he'd split up with Michelle."

Dawn paused for breath, her bottom lip wobbling. Julia plucked a tissue from the box on the table and passed it over.

"Thank you," she said before blowing her nose. "I can't believe I'm telling you all of this. I've never told anyone. When Theo arrived here the afternoon after I did, he looked at me like he did in that cinema twenty-three years ago. It was like no time had passed, and he was seeing me for the first time. After everything that had happened with Ethan, I couldn't help myself. I needed to feel safe, and Theo always did that. I think it's taken me all of this time to realise I've been in love with Theo, and I've just been projecting that onto Ethan because they share a face. It was never some seedy affair. Our lips hadn't touched in twenty-three years until we came here."

"I believe you," Julia said, absorbing everything carefully.

"When the housekeeper was pushed down the stairs, I was with -"

Barker suddenly burst through the door, a look of terror on his pale face. Both women jumped up in an instant and ran out to the entrance hall.

"Where is he?" Dawn cried, her hands disappearing up into her hair. "Barker, please tell –"

Julia and Dawn's eyes both wandered to the ajar basement door at the same time, both knowing what was down there.

Dawn ran towards the basement, followed by Julia and Barker. They both ran down the stone steps into the freezing room under the manor. Under the single bulb stood Heather, Casper, Bella, Conrad, Theo, Dot, Jessie, and Billy. They were all crowded around something in the middle of the room.

"We've called an ambulance," Dot explained, stepping back to show Ethan on the floor, a bottle of pills clutched in his hand. "I – I think it's too late."

Julia pushed through the crowd as Dawn

screeched against Barker's chest. Julia pulled the blue bottle from his hand, pills scattered around his bald head.

"*Beta blockers*," Julia cried, tossing the bottle to the ground. "They're Hilary's blood pressure pills! She was looking for them. I think he's had a heart attack."

Julia pressed her finger to his neck, a faint pulse beating against her fingertips.

"Give him some room," Julia cried as she straightened out Ethan's limp body. "He needs CPR."

"*Dad?*" Bella cried, looking at Theo. "You work for the St. John's Ambulance. You should know this."

Theo stared down at his brother, his eyes wide as though he did not know where he was.

"*Theo!*" Dawn cried. "*Do something!*"

Julia stared up expectantly at Ethan's twin brother, but his eyes stared right through her. He doubled back and pushed through the crowd, knocking Casper clean off his feet before running up the stairs.

"*Step back!*" Dot announced, pushing Julia out of the way. "I saw a documentary about this."

Dot locked her hands together and began to

pump down on the man's chest with more force than looked possible from the slender old woman. When nobody else jumped forward claiming to have superior knowledge to Dot, Julia stepped back and clutched Barker's hand, her ears pricked and listening out for the ambulance sirens.

CHAPTER 14

"You might have just saved his life," the paramedic called to Dot as they rushed Ethan out of the manor on a stretcher after defibrillating his heart in the basement. "It's a good job somebody had CPR training, or he'd be a goner."

"It was nothing," Dot said with a proud smile as she brushed down the pleats in her knee-length navy blue skirt. "First-aid is a passion of mine."

"I thought she said she'd just watched a documentary?" Jessie whispered, to which Dot stamped on her foot. "*Ouch!*"

"I'm going with him," Dawn cried, bolting to the door as the paramedics rushed him towards the ambulance directly in front of the manor doors. "He needs me."

"You need to stay," Julia called out, the words almost catching in her throat. "You can't leave."

"He's my *husband!*"

"There's nothing you can do," Barker said, pulling Dawn back from the door. "You can't leave until this is figured out."

"I don't care about this *stupid* investigation," she cried, thrashing against Barker as the paramedics closed the ambulance doors. "He can't be alone."

"You're not leaving," DS Christie said firmly, standing in the doorway. "I'm sorry, but you're still a suspect until we say otherwise."

"I'll go, Auntie Dawn," Bella said, rushing towards the door. "I'll make sure he's okay."

Barker nodded at DS Christie. He stepped to the side and let Bella rush after the ambulance. She banged on the back doors until they opened up. They sped off before she had even fully closed them behind her.

Julia looked at Jessie and Billy, who were standing hand in hand in the archway to the sitting room. Conrad was slumped in the corner of the stairs crying to himself, and Heather was massaging Casper's stump in the kitchen, his prosthetic sitting on the counter.

"I can't believe Theo froze up like that," Barker whispered after letting go of Dawn. "He looked scared."

Dawn stumbled past Conrad and made her way carefully up the stairs. She opened her bedroom door, slamming it behind her.

"Why would he take an overdose?" DS Christie asked, walking up behind them with crossed arms. "I don't understand."

"It's not the first time," Julia explained, pulling the note from her pocket. "The first note was longer than this one. I suddenly feel like it has the answers we need to figure this out."

"At least we know where Hilary's pills went," Dot exclaimed. "I do hope the old girl is okay. I don't like her all that much, but when you get to a certain age, you want to go out in a blaze of glory, not after being pushed down the stairs. I think I might call Brian to see how she's doing."

Dot shuffled past them, shaking her head softly. She cast an eye to the leg on the table, but she did not make a comment. She placed a cup next to it and began preparing a pot of tea.

"What's going on?" Katie cried from the top of the stairs, her eyes half closed, and her hands on her bump. "The sirens woke me up."

"Ethan had a heart attack," Julia explained. "Go back to bed. There's nothing you can do."

Katie sighed heavily before turning and waddling back to her bedroom. Julia could not imagine spending the final days of pregnancy in such a tense situation. Sue had had the right idea getting Neil to pick her up before things turned serious. She pulled her phone from her pocket to see if her sister had messaged her, but it was on the picture of Casper's footprints on the carpet. She flicked to the image of the fleshy blur.

"What do you see, Billy?" Julia asked, eager for a fresh opinion.

"Looks like a bum," he offered as he squinted under the shadow of his cap. "Is it Barker's?"

"No, it's not!" Barker snapped before turning back to the study. "I'm going to go over all these notes. Maybe I've missed something."

Jessie and Billy wandered into the sitting room,

AGATHA FROST

while Conrad leaned against the bannister, his eyes fluttering. Leaving them alone, Julia wandered up the stairs and walked into Dawn's bedroom without invitation.

She was curled up on top of the ornate four-poster bed in the dark, her eyes blank and unblinking as she clung to a giant fluffy pillow. Julia closed the door behind her and flicked on the bedside lamp. Dawn squinted, but she did not look up at Julia.

"They're going to do their best to save him," Julia whispered as she brushed Dawn's pale hair from her face. "They got here quickly."

Dawn shrugged. Whether it was a shrug to indicate she did not care if her husband would live or die, or she did not care about what Julia had to say, Julia did not know.

"There's something I want to ask you," Julia said calmly. "Something I think you've known for twenty-three years, but never allowed yourself to say out loud."

Dawn closed her eyes slowly before springing them back open again. She slid up the silk duvet cover and leaned against the headrest, the giant pillow clutched in front of her. She suddenly looked less like a woman in her forties, and more like a girl

Bella's age.

"No," she said, her voice muffled by the pillow. "*No, no, no.* It's not true."

"Is there a chance that Luke was Theo's son?" Julia asked bluntly, resting her hand against Dawn's sock, the only part of her she could reach. "And is there a chance Luke knew?"

"No, you've got this all wrong," Dawn said, edging her foot away as she clenched her eyes. "Luke *is* – I mean, he *was* Ethan's. You can't prove otherwise."

"You're right," Julia said as she carefully crawled up the bed to lean against the headrest with Dawn. "I can't. But you know in your heart of hearts if he was. What month was Luke born?"

"September."

"And you got pregnant in February?" Julia asked. "Or did you find out you were pregnant in February, and were you really already pregnant when Theo ended things over the phone?"

"I ended up in bed with Ethan when I went to give Theo the present," Dawn said defiantly. "*That's* when I got pregnant."

Just from the wobble in the woman's voice, Julia knew she was trying to convince herself, just like she had been for the last two decades.

"You know as well as I do that you didn't get pregnant with Ethan the first time, and then never again for the next decade. You said yourself you tried up until your thirties to conceive with him."

"We were *unlucky*," Dawn whispered, turning to Julia with hopeful eyes. "Luck, Julia. Nothing more."

"But is there a chance?" Julia asked, leaning her head against the wooden headrest to stare up at the glittering light in the ceiling. "There was an overlap. You can't know for certain, can you?"

Julia rolled her eyes to Dawn, who could only offer a shake of her head.

"Is that what Ethan's first note was about?" Julia asked. "Did he know?"

"What?"

"The suicide note," Julia said. "The one Jessie tore up."

"I *told* you, that has *nothing* to do with this."

"So, it wasn't about Luke?"

"Why would it be?" she barked, suddenly sitting up and narrowing her eyes sternly on Julia. "I told you, it's got nothing to do with what happened to Luke."

"What was Ethan guilty about?" Julia asked, thinking back to the second note. "What is haunting him so much that he tried to take his own life for a second time?"

Dawn reached into her pocket to pull out the note. It was crinkled, and the tape had started to peel off. She clung to it for the longest time, her reluctance to let Julia in on the secret palpable.

"I had no idea about this," Dawn said, opening up the note to look down at the scribbled writing. "He never told me a thing. I've been trying to forget I ever read this. I only brought it here because I haven't been able to part with it since. I hoped if I just clung to it and nobody found out, we could go back to normal and pretend none of it ever happened."

With shaky hands, Dawn held out the note, the paper rustling. Julia leaned across the bed and flicked on the second bedside lamp, flooding the grand room with more yellowy light. She accepted the letter, gulped hard, and began to read:

'*To Dawn.*

I'm so sorry to do this to you. After reading this, you'll understand. I hope you don't hate me too much, it's just impossible to live with this secret for another day. I've clung onto it for three long years, and there has not been a day that I haven't tortured myself about it. You know me.

I put on a brave face for the world, but no more. The lie has to end, and I hope this family can feel some peace when they know the truth. I hope you can all forgive me and understand why I did it.

Bethany wasn't driving the car, nor was she drunk. I was driving, and I was the drunk one. She left the party for some fresh air, and she saw me in my car. She came over and got in, and started talking to me. You know I've always been able to hide how I feel. I lied and said I'd had a couple of drinks, but I was okay to drive. She said she wanted some cigarettes. She'd only just taken it up but was scared to smoke in front of her dad. I said I'd drive her to buy some if she promised to quit. The second I pulled out of the car park, I knew I'd made a mistake, but I kept going. The nearest shop was closed, but I knew about that little shop on the edge of Burgwood Forest that was open twenty-four hours. Remember it? It was the one we used to buy ice pops from in the middle of the night when Luke was teething. I was going too fast. She told me to slow down, but I told her she was safe with me. 'Uncle Ethan will look after you'. A dog ran out into the road. I should have just hit it and carried on. It would have been better than what happened. I veered off. I smashed into that tree. I was wearing my seatbelt, but Bethany wasn't. I hadn't even noticed. I should have checked before I set off.

BIRTHDAY CAKE AND BODIES

Everything hurt, but I somehow got out of the car. I walked around to the passenger seat, but she was dead. I didn't want to be blamed for what happened, so I switched seats. I knew I couldn't look at any of you ever again if you thought I'd done this. She was so thin and tiny. It was like picking up a doll. I put her behind the wheel and strapped myself into the passenger seat, and then I started screaming for help. A car drove past a minute later and called an ambulance. I couldn't bring myself to look at her. I wanted to close my eyes and die too. I wish I had. I killed her, and her final act in life was to take the blame for me. I don't know if there's an afterlife, but I suspect I won't be going to the same place as sweet Bethany. I deserve that.

Believe me when I say that I'm sorry.

There's a couple of thousand pounds in the safe for a funeral. The combination is Luke's birthday. I love you, Dawn. I always have, and I always will.

I was never truly yours, was I?

Ethan.'

A tear ran from Julia's eye and landed on the paper, spoiling the ink. She let the letter fall from her hands as though it was made from lead. She turned to Dawn, who had resumed staring blankly into space.

"That was on Bethany's three-year anniversary," Dawn said with a sudden calmness. "It's been hell on Earth since that day. Ethan tried to resume his usual act of pretending everything was fine, but I could see right through it. I'd pulled back the curtain, and seen that the wizard was nothing more than a pathetic, little man. I was disgusted by what he had done. I came here *hoping* to see Theo. I wanted the good brother again. I was tired of living a lie."

"Where were you when Luke died?" Julia asked. "Were you with Theo?"

Dawn nodded. She tossed the pillow across the bed, sat up, and crossed her legs. She began to fiddle with the frayed edge of her black jeans, mesmerised by the thread as she pulled on it.

"Ethan was asleep," Dawn explained. "I slipped out and went to see Theo. It was like no time had passed. It just erupted in seconds. He made me feel things I hadn't felt since the last time he'd touched me."

"What time was that?" Julia asked, thinking

back to the timeline in her mind. "Between five and six?"

"I don't know," Dawn admitted, her light brows furrowing over her eyes. "I just remember seeing the clock in the bathroom when I was freshening up. It was about twenty to six."

"How long were you in there?"

"I had a quick shower," she admitted. "I didn't want to go back to Ethan smelling like his brother. I think I was only gone for about fifteen minutes."

"Where was the letter?"

"In my handbag."

"And where was your handbag?" Julia asked. "Did you take it with you, or did you leave it with Ethan?"

Dawn turned to face Julia, her eyes crinkling as she thought.

"I took it with me, I think," she said. "Yes, that's right. I went back in to get it because I remember seeing Theo putting his contact lenses back in. He used to wear glasses when we were kids. That was the only way I could tell them apart before Ethan broke his nose in the crash."

Julia jumped up, her head spinning. She pushed her hands up into her hair as the pieces finally slotted into place. Like kicking a door open and flooding her mind with light, all of the things she knew suddenly lined up and made sense. She pulled out her phone and looked down at the picture of the fleshy blur.

"It's not what they think," she whispered to herself. "It's a *head*. A *bald head*. Dawn, where is Theo?"

"I – I don't know," she said, shaking her head as she stood up. "W-What are you saying?"

Julia had no time to explain, she pulled open the door, and looked up and down the hallway, her heart stopping when she saw Katie hobbling out of her bedroom, hands clutching her stomach, a wet patch on her pink silk nightie.

"*Julia*," she moaned, her voice tight as sweat poured down her red face. "It's *happening*. The baby is coming."

CHAPTER 15

Julia had never witnessed childbirth before, but it was nothing like she would ever have expected. Her romantic mental image of the miracle had been replaced with something much louder and messier. As she looked down at the tiny dark haired baby in Katie's arms, its face bright red as its tiny lungs bellowed out, she could not believe how fast everything had happened.

"*Katie?*" Brian cried as he ran into the hospital room, sweat dripping down his face. "I've only just got your message, Julia. Have I -,"

Brian's eyes drifted down to his new son. He pushed his hands up into his thick hair, his lips shaking with a confused smile.

"Your wife did amazingly," Katie's midwife said as she smiled down at the baby. "You should be proud of her."

"I *should* have been here," he said, his eyes fixed on the baby. "Katie, I'm so -"

"I wasn't alone," Katie croaked, her voice weak from all the screaming. "Julia was here the whole time. She didn't leave my side."

Katie gave Julia's hand a little squeeze, softer than she had while pushing.

"I was happy to be here," Julia said.

Brian lifted the baby from Katie's arms and held him against his chest. His eyes watered as soon as he looked down at his son's scrunched up face.

"Hello, little man," he whispered, tears streaming down his lined cheeks. "Were you in a hurry to meet us?"

"*Vinnie,*" Katie said. "I want to call him Vinnie, after my dad."

"Vinnie it is," Brian said as he carefully rocked

the baby. "It suits him."

"Vinnie *Jules* Wellington-South," Katie said, squeezing Julia's hand again. "He wouldn't be here without his big sister."

Julia's eyes welled up before she had time to wipe them dry. Over the last hour in the delivery room, she had grown closer to Katie than she ever thought conceivable. It would be impossible for them not to be connected on a completely new level after sharing something so important.

"How did this happen so fast?" Brian asked as he passed Vinnie back to Katie. "I thought it was supposed to be slow? We had a birthing plan."

"There wasn't any time for the candles and whale music, Mr South," the midwife said. "Like you said, sometimes the baby is just in a hurry."

"I started having contractions in bed," Katie explained. "They were far apart and faint at first. I thought it was Braxton Hicks from the stress, but then they got worse, and my waters broke, and –"

"We came straight here," Julia explained. "I kept trying to call you, but it went through to voicemail every time."

"I was asleep," he admitted, red rings around his eyes. "I was waiting for Hilary to get out of surgery. I'd still be asleep if one of the nurses hadn't shaken me awake to tell me they were finished."

"How is she?" Julia asked, suddenly remembering about the housekeeper's tumble. "Is she awake?"

"Not yet," Brian said, his eyes conveying something his lips did not want to in front of his exhausted wife. "I'm sure she'll come around soon."

"I think it's time for you to give your first feed, Katie," the midwife said, flicking through a chart as she smiled politely at Julia. "The sooner, the better."

"I'll leave you two alone," Julia said, letting go of Katie's hand for the first time since being rushed into the tiny room. "You did a great job, Katie."

"Thank you, Julia," she said with a soft smile. "Thank you for not leaving me."

"I would never have left you," Julia assured her. "We're family, remember?"

Julia bowed her head and slipped into the sterile corridor, the fluorescent lighting blinding her from above. She caught her reflection in the glass window of the room opposite Katie's. Her curls were scruffy and still had cake icing in them, her eyes were like dark saucers, and her navy blouse was covered in more stains than she cared to try to identify.

"Julia," Brian whispered, slipping through the door and into the corridor. "Thank you for being here."

"Honestly, it was nothing."

"No, I really mean it, kid," he said, cupping her cheek in his hand. "She's been worrying herself sick about this for weeks. She couldn't have got through that without you by her side."

Julia looked through the window. Despite Katie's damp matted hair and drained face, Julia knew Katie would never be the same woman again. She looked at the baby's dark hair poking out of the blanket before the midwife pulled the curtain across the meshed glass.

"I have a little brother," she said, as though it had only just sunk in. "A baby brother."

"Everything has just changed," he said with a wink. "I never thought I'd be a dad again, especially at this age, but here we are. Stranger things have happened, right?"

"Speaking of which," Julia said, lowering her voice as a nurse hurried past. "How's Hilary really?"

Brian let go of her cheek as he inhaled heavily. Julia could tell it was not good news.

"She survived the surgery," he started, looking up and down the empty corridor. "The surgeon said *if* she wakes up, there might be *complications*."

"Complications?"

"Brain damage." Brian gulped hard. "She hit her head pretty hard on that marble floor when she fell."

"She was pushed," Julia said, remembering exactly what had been happening over the last twelve hours. "Dad, I need to get back to the manor. I know who is behind all of this."

"I'm sure I saw one of those twins being brought in on a stretcher when I was in intensive care," Brian said, his brow tensing. "Could have been someone else."

"Ethan is here?" The corridor walls shrunk around her. "I'll call you later."

Without another word, Julia hurried down the corridor and burst out into an empty reception area. The clock on the wall boasted that it was almost four in the morning, letting her know she had lost valuable hours. She ran over to the giant map on the wall. She ran her finger across the list of departments until she landed on 'Intensive Care', which was on level five. Would she lose even more time visiting Ethan to make sure he was okay?

She pulled out her phone, her battery dangerously low. She quickly scrolled to Jessie's name, relieved when she picked up in seconds.

"Did she have it?" Jessie whispered. "Everyone's fallen asleep. Everything is fine here before you ask.

No more deaths."

"The baby is fine," Julia said. "Healthy eight pounds. She's called him Vinnie."

"*Vinnie?*" Jessie cried. "What a dumb name. Sounds like a mob gangster."

"Is Dawn there?"

"She's in her room," Jessie said. "Fast asleep. I keep checking. Billy is keeping watch on the door with the police guy."

"And Theo?"

"Hasn't been seen since he bailed on us in the basement," Jessie said. "Hang on, there's a nurse trying to get in at the front door. I think it's Vincent's NHS carer. The officer is blocking her. I'll call you back. Oh, and Julia, one more thing –"

Jessie never got to tell Julia her '*one more thing*'. The phone beeped and the screen blackened.

"*Dammit!*" she cried, stuffing the dead phone back into her pocket. "Why didn't I call Barker first?"

Realising she was the only one who had figured out exactly what had happened to Hilary and Luke, Julia looked at the payphone on the wall, wondering if she should call the police. Would she even make any sense? Would they believe her?

Julia doubled back and called for the lift. When

she was inside, her heart pounded as she drifted up to the top floor of the giant hospital. The doors slid open onto a dimly lit blue corridor. The seriousness of the illnesses and conditions was obvious from the absence of any noise aside from the steady hum of beeping machines. Julia spotted a young woman behind a curved reception desk reading a magazine. She let out a long yawn before blinking heavily and turning the page.

"Hello," Julia whispered as she approached the desk. "I was wondering if you could help me. I'm looking for Ethan Brown. He was brought in here a couple of hours ago. I think he might have had a heart attack."

"Visiting starts at eight," the woman said as she stifled another yawn. "You'll be better coming back then."

"Would you be able to tell me if he's okay?" Julia asked, glancing at the computer. "I just want to know that he's alive."

"Are you related?" she asked, arching a brow as she slapped her magazine shut.

"Sort of," Julia said with a shrug as the nurse's hand drifted towards the computer mouse. "I'm his brother's girlfriend."

"Then I can't tell you anything," she said, her

hand going back to the magazine. "Patient confidentiality. I'm sorry, miss."

Julia nodded her understanding and reluctantly backed away from the desk. She stared down the long corridor, a dozen doors on either side leading into private rooms each with a window. A doctor walked out of one with a clipboard and into another, closing the door softly behind him.

She called the lift and waited as it shuddered back up to the top floor. The bell pinged and the doors rattled open. Julia stepped in, but the sound of a kettle boiling pricked her ears. The button on the kettle clicked, and the chair behind the reception desk creaked. The nurse wandered into the back room, checking the watch attached to the breast pocket of her blue uniform as she walked towards the kettle.

Julia did not waste a single second bothering to formulate a plan; she knew she had nothing to lose. Letting the lift doors close behind her, she darted down the corridor as softly as she could so her shoes did not squeak on the polished blue linoleum floor. She whizzed past the desk holding her breath, daring to glance at the nurse as she emptied a sachet of dried soup into a large mug.

Julia walked down the middle of the corridor,

looking through each room window on either side, hoping to see the bald head. She stopped in her tracks, and she saw a very familiar face with a large bandage wrapped around her head. Julia approached the window and stared at the tube sticking out of Hilary's mouth, her chest rising and falling with the aid of the giant machines surrounding her.

Swallowing the lump in her throat, Julia tore herself away from the window to continue on her journey down the dark corridor. Relief surged through her when she saw Ethan's head shining under a soft wall light, a similar tube poking out of his parted lips.

"You're alive," she whispered, nodding carefully as she allowed herself to smile. "Thank God, you're alive."

Julia stepped towards the door, instantly jumping back again when she saw the glimmer of a white coat in the dark corner of the room. She held her breath, hoping the doctor had not seen her. She almost turned on her heels to make her way back to the lift, satisfied that Ethan was alive, until she spotted another familiar bald head. Horror rose up in Julia when she noticed that the man in the white coat was wearing jeans, trainers, and was holding a large white pillow in his hands.

She watched in shock as Theo approached his brother with the pillow. She wanted to scream out to alert everyone, but something stopped her. If she caused a panic, would she be able to prove her theory? She patted her phone, cursing under her breath when she remembered its dead battery.

Julia waited until Theo was hovering over his twin brother's face with the pillow before making her entrance. She slipped silently into the room, her heart banging against her ribcage.

"Stop it, Theo," she said, her voice shaking out of control. "There's been enough death."

Theo darted around, the pillow still in his hands. His eyes widened when he realised it was Julia and not one of the hospital staff. She glanced at the panic button over the bed, gulping down her fear as she collected her thoughts.

"Julia," he said, forcing a strange, cold laugh. "I was just making sure my brother was comfortable."

"In a white coat?"

"They wouldn't let me in," he said, fluffing the pillow before tossing it onto a large chair. "What are you doing here?"

"I came to see if Ethan was okay."

"Me too," Theo said quickly, staring deep into Julia's eyes. "I felt bad about freezing in the basement. I forgot my training in the heat of the moment. I was hoping he would be awake so we could talk."

"Or, so you could look him in the eyes while you killed him?" Julia asked, taking a step forward so that the bed was separating them, but also keeping close to the door. "Would I be right in thinking you have your contact lenses in this time?"

Theo's jaw gritted as his spine stiffened. The corners of his eyes crinkled as he stared at Julia in the dim light, half of his pale face cast in shadow. All of a sudden, there was more than a broken nose separating the twins; there was a look that unsettled Julia to the core.

"I don't know what you're talking about," Theo said drily. "You've clearly added two and two together and got five. Why would I want to kill my brother?"

"Because you know," Julia said, making sure to maintain his cold gaze. "You know what he did to Bethany. You read Dawn's letter, and you were so angry that you immediately wanted to kill him for his deception."

Theo glanced down at Ethan, and then at the door. Julia knew if he tried to run there would be little she could do to stop him. To her surprise, he relaxed a little and folded his arms tightly across the stolen white coat.

"Except Ethan didn't die," he said calmly, his tone smug. "Luke did."

"Eyesight is a funny thing," Julia said, glancing at the panic button again. "I've needed to take an eye test all year, but I've been putting it off. I think I need reading glasses, but I don't want to admit that I'm getting old. Of course, poor vision isn't a sign of getting old for all of us, is it? Some of us are born with bad eyesight. The first time we spoke, you were taking your contact lenses out because they were irritating you."

"So?"

"How bad is your vision?" Julia asked, squinting at Theo's eyes. "Are you wearing them now? I suppose you are. You figured out this was your brother, even though the room is dark, unlike at the manor."

Theo's eyes narrowed to slits on Julia. His Adam's apple bobbed down his stubble covered neck and back up again, as though he was swallowing sand.

"Dawn was right about you," he whispered through tight lips. "*Little Miss Know It All.*"

"You took your contact lenses out when you

slept with Dawn yesterday afternoon," Julia continued, her voice rising as she glanced at the monitor, Ethan's heart rate suddenly quickening. "When she went to freshen up, you found the letter in her handbag. Maybe you were looking for it, or maybe you knocked over her bag and it fell out, and curiosity got the better of you. Either way, you realised Ethan was responsible for Bethany's death in a way you never knew. You blamed him from the start, I know that much, but to find out that he framed her for the crash, I can imagine what that did to you. You were so angry, you didn't even stop to put your contacts back in. You walked out of your bedroom and into Ethan and Dawn's bedroom next door, but you didn't know that Ethan and Dawn had swapped rooms with Luke because Dawn wanted the bigger bed. Neither did I until Casper told me. You wrapped your hands around your nephew's neck, thinking he was your brother, and you squeezed every last ounce of life out of his twenty-two-year-old body. I wish my phone wasn't dead because I'd be able to show you the picture he took of the top of your head while you were murdering him.

"You left him there in the sheets, went back to your bedroom, and pretended nothing had happened. You were putting in your contact lenses when Dawn came back to get her bag, and she was none the wiser. How did you hide what you had just done? You must be a good actor. I couldn't imagine murdering someone and then pretending everything was fine seconds later."

"Pretending everything was fine?" Theo replied, resting his hands against the edge of the bed and leaning across Ethan's lifeless body. "The only thing I was hiding was my smile. I thought I'd killed the man responsible for murdering my daughter. I was over the moon, Julia."

"Until you found out you'd killed Luke, not Ethan," Julia continued. "Did you feel a scrap of remorse then?"

Theo's lids flickered, but he did not say a word.

"I think you did," Julia said with a firm nod. "You were upset when I spoke to you. You weren't faking that. Maybe you were crying for Bethany, but I think you realised your mistake. Luke might not have been an angel, but he was innocent when it came to Bethany's death."

"That boy was anything *but* innocent," Theo said suddenly. "I know what he did to Casper and Heather, and I figured out his seedy affair with Conrad the minute I arrived. They barely even tried to hide the looks they were giving each other."

"Still, not really grounds for murder, are they?" Julia said, taking a step forward to rest her hands on the edge of the bed so they were face to face. "You messed up. You killed the wrong person, and then you backed away. You let everything happen around you, hoping nobody would connect the dots. I wouldn't have if I hadn't seen you and Dawn kissing. That was the one piece of the jigsaw that pointed me to you when I had all of the information in front of me."

Theo straightened up and glanced at the door again. He parted his feet, planting them firmly on the floor. He cocked his head back and looked down at Julia as though he were thinking about what to do with her.

"How *does* Barker live with you?" he muttered darkly. "I always thought he had taste."

"Why Hilary?" Julia asked, ignoring him. "What did she say to you?"

"The nosey bat approached me about the affair," he said with a strained laugh, the veins in his neck looking fit to burst. "Said she was dusting the skirting boards when Dawn left my room to go to the bathroom with a sheet wrapped around her. I knew she'd figure it out sooner or later if anyone found out about that letter. Maybe she shouldn't have confronted me at the top of that nice long staircase."

"Do you not have *any* guilt?" Julia asked desperately as she shook her head. "Do you not *regret* almost killing an innocent woman?"

"Almost?" he asked, the surprise loud and clear. "So, she's survived then? The only regret I have is not finishing off my brother while I had the chance. I should have choked out his last breath the moment I realised I had killed the wrong idiot."

"Please," Ethan croaked through the pipe in his throat, his swollen lids fluttering open. "Do it."

Theo turned to his brother, his eyes filling with rage. His top lip snarled up while his bottom wobbled.

"She was a *child*," Theo sneered. "*You* took her life away from me."

Ethan attempted to say something else, but the pipe choked him, making him gag. His face contoured as he tried to cough, but his body would not allow it.

Theo snatched up the pillow with lightning fast reflexes. Without taking a second to think about it, he pressed the thick pillow over his twin's face, the pipe to his mouth splitting open. One of the machines beeped loudly as Ethan's body thrashed against the bed.

"*Get off him*!" Julia cried, running around the bed to grab Theo. "You've done *enough*!"

Theo's elbow struck the side of Julia's head, sending her crashing against the chair. She landed on all fours, the room spinning around her as a splitting pain cracked behind her eyes. She groaned out, suddenly feeling sick to her stomach, her ears ringing.

"You're a *monster*!" Theo cried. "This is what you *deserve*, brother!"

Julia crawled towards the wall as the floor swayed from side to side. She slapped a hand up to the window ledge, and with every ounce of strength she had left, she dragged herself up to her feet. As though knowing the answer before thinking about it, she picked up the heavy chair, her vision blurred. As the room spun around her, she lifted it clumsily above her head, stumbling on the spot, the pain all-consuming. With one swift crash, she sent the chair flying down on Theo's head. He folded in half, rolling down his brother's torso before slipping down onto the floor. Julia stepped over the broken chair, yanked the pillow off Ethan's face, and slapped the panic button.

"What the -" the doctor gasped as he burst into the room. "What's going on?"

"Call the police," Julia said, clutching the side of her head as Ethan blinked and gasped for air. "And get some bandage tape. I need to tie up the man on the floor while you check on Ethan."

***

"HONESTLY, I'M FINE," JULIA SAID AS the doctor lifted up her left eyelid to shine the bright light directly into her pupil. "It's nothing painkillers won't fix."

"*Julia?*" Barker cried as he bolted through the lift doors and towards the reception desk where Doctor Husain was checking her over. "I drove as fast as I could. Are you okay? What's happened to you?"

"I'm fine," Julia said, brushing the doctor's hands away as he checked on her other eye. "It was just a slight elbow to the head. I've taken worse."

Barker wrapped his arms tightly around her, cradling her like a baby. She allowed herself to sink into his musky scent, undeniably glad that everything was over.

"*Get off!*" Theo cried as two officers dragged him down the corridor towards the lift. "You have *no* evidence! You *can't* do this! She's *crazy*! She's making it *all* up!"

"You make me sick, Theo," Barker said, pulling away from Julia as they passed. "Don't go easy on him, boys. He killed my nephew."

"I'm your *brother*!" Theo yelled, screaming over his shoulder. "Ethan *killed* Bethany! *He* was driving!"

Barker looked down at Julia for an explanation. She nodded to let him know it was true. She slid off the chair behind the desk and wandered into the middle of the corridor as the officers pushed Theo into the lift. She stepped forward as the doors began to slide, locking eyes with the murderer.

"You probably already know there's a strong possibility that Luke was your son," Julia said calmly. "Good luck living with that, Theo."

His eyes widened and his mouth twisted tightly into something that closely resembled a rabid dog. He thrashed against the officers as the doors closed, spitting and foaming at the mouth.

"I think we need a long conversation," Barker said as he wrapped his arm around Julia's waist as she stared at the lift doors. "It seems that I've missed a lot, as usual."

"Julia?" Doctor Husain called from the doorway of Ethan's room. "Mr Brown is asking for you."

Julia walked down the corridor, glancing at Hilary as she did; there was no change. She slipped into Ethan's room, glad to see the tube gone from his mouth. Despite everything, he looked aware and alive; that was all Julia cared about.

She sat on the edge of the bed and picked up one of his limp hands. After giving Doctor Husain a look to let him know to leave them alone for a minute, she turned to Ethan and smiled down at him.

"I heard everything," he whispered, his voice hoarse. "I thought I was dreaming."

"I wish it had all been a dream," she said with a sad smile. "You've been through a lot, haven't you?"

"How do I live with myself?" Ethan asked, clenching his eyes as the tears started. "I killed my niece, and I framed her."

"It was an accident," Julia reassured him. "Tell the police what happened. You never intended to kill her. You were drunk. You panicked. She was dead either way."

"I should never have driven."

"We can't change the past."

"I'm no better than Theo."

"You are." Julia squeezed his hand firmly. "You never *wanted* to kill anyone. Theo murdered Luke in cold blood, and attempted to murder you and Hilary. You're nothing alike."

Ethan nodded, his lips twisting as more tears leaked out of the corner of his eyes. Julia let go of his hand and backed away from the door before the conversation drifted onto Luke. Even if Ethan had his suspicions about the paternity of his late son, it was not Julia's place to speculate, especially since they would now never know the truth.

"Will he live?" Barker asked the doctor when Julia returned to his side. "Give it to me straight."

"He suffered a considerable cardiac arrest," the doctor said quietly. "And he took a very large overdose of beta blockers. We'll keep a close eye on him for the rest of the night, which will be rough for him as he recovers and gets the pills out of his system. Until then, it's a waiting game."

Doctor Husain smiled sympathetically at Julia before slipping past her and into the room behind the reception desk, where the nurse was sipping her instant soup, her eyes wide and blank, no doubt from the shock.

"What now?" Barker asked, wrapping his arm around her shoulder.

"Take me home," she whispered, resting her head against his broad chest as they wandered slowly towards the lift doors. "There's only one Brown man I want to be with when the sun rises."

CHAPTER 16

J ulia's eyes did not open until close to noon, and that was only because the salty scent of bacon tickled her nostrils.

"Morning," Barker whispered as he set the tray on his side of the bed, which was unusually neat and tidy. "I thought I'd return the favour from yesterday morning."

"That was only yesterday?" Julia groaned, rubbing her eyes as she sat up in bed, still in the same blouse she had worn all day yesterday. "Any updates?"

"Theo has confessed to everything you suspected." Barker sat on the edge of the bed, placed his pillow across Julia's knee, and rested the plate on top. "But for now, all that matters is this fry-up I lovingly made. I even have the oil burns to prove it."

Julia wolfed down her breakfast alone while Barker watched the news on his new television in the sitting room. It was the first thing she had eaten since dinner the previous day, aside from cookies and a mouthful of birthday cake. When she was finished, Mowgli jumped onto the bed to snatch the bacon fat from her plate. She stared ahead at the mirror on her dressing table, her hair wild and bushy.

"What a day," she whispered as she stuffed her feet into her warm sheepskin slippers. "I can smell myself, boy, and that's never a good sign."

Mowgli did not look up from chewing his bacon fat on the other side of the room.

After a long, hot, soapy shower, Julia dried her hair, applied some mascara, and selected one of her favourite pastel blue vintage dresses. She loved the way the white trim on the hem and the neckline popped against her pale skin. It was still cold outside, but from the beautiful countryside view she had from her bedroom window, it looked like it was going to be a dry day. When she was ready to face the world, she stepped back and assessed herself in the mirror.

"That's better."

Leaving Mowgli to lick the oil and butter off her plate, she wandered into the kitchen and made herself a cup of tea.

"Where's Jessie?" Julia asked Barker as she sipped her peppermint and liquorice tea. "Is she still asleep?"

"She's been at the café since eight," Barker said, barely tearing his eyes away from his new giant TV. "She said she didn't want to let you down."

"She didn't have to," Julia muttered to herself. "How's Ethan?"

"Alive," Barker said, turning off the TV before tossing the remote onto the coffee table. "I called him this morning, and he said he was going to tell the police everything about Bethany when he gives his statement."

"Do you think they'll put him in prison?"

"Honestly?" Barker said, standing up and

stretching out. The dark shadows under his eyes let Julia know he had not had as good a night's sleep as she had. "It depends on the judge, but considering what has happened with Luke and the lengths Theo went to for revenge, I think he might escape prison. There's the dangerous driving and the manslaughter, and then there's the perverting the course of justice on top of that. Only time will tell. Between you and me, I'm not sure how to feel about it. Knowing he did that to Bethany after she died makes me feel sick."

"He was desperate," Julia said as she stuffed her feet into her shoes. "I don't think they were the actions of a rationally thinking man. He needs counselling above anything."

"Let's hope he accepts it this time," Barker said, kissing Julia on the forehead as he passed to grab his jacket from the hook. "He's turned it down every time it's been offered, all the way back to being a teenager. I thought he'd fought his demons, but I think he just got better at hiding them."

"I wonder where it all stems from," Julia thought aloud as she shrugged on her pink pea coat. "I suppose mental health is never that simple, is it?"

"I know he grew up in Theo's shadow. Theo was the popular, funny, intelligent one, and Ethan loved his video games. Getting Dawn was the one good thing that happened to him up until that point, but as it turned out, he never even had that for real."

"Have you heard anything about Hilary?" Julia asked, her heart still hurting for the housekeeper. "My dad was talking about brain damage last night."

"She's awake, and she can talk, so that's something. The doctor said it was too early to rule anything out, but she's survived. She's lucky to be alive."

With Julia's car still at the manor, they drove into the village in Barker's. Julia was not surprised to see the café completely packed when they pulled up outside.

"*Julia!* What happened?"

"Tell us *everything!*"

"*Another* murder in Peridale?"

"Are you sure you want to be part of *that* family?"

After an afternoon of answering questions and dispelling rumours, Julia was more than happy to lock the door at half past five.

"You've just got a text message," Jessie said, picking up Julia's phone from behind the counter. "It's from Brian. They're home with the baby."

"Do you want to go and meet your sort-of

uncle?" Julia asked with a smirk. "I'm sure he'll be bossing you around in a couple of years."

"He can try."

Without Julia's car, they strolled up to Peridale Manor in the dark. The police roadblock had been moved, and someone had parked Julia's beloved car neatly next to the orange camper.

"*Julia!*" Casper exclaimed when they slipped through the door without knocking. "We were just leaving, weren't we, Heather?"

"Yes," she said sheepishly, both of their bags in her hands. "I owe you an apology, Julia. I was a little too firm with you yesterday, and I've regretted it ever since. I know you were only trying to help."

"It's forgotten," Julia said, winking at the short woman. "Do you know what you're going to do next?"

"I have a feeling things will be just fine," Casper said, his arm wobbling as he leaned his entire weight on his cane. "It turns out your father knows the fella who took my medals off me for a bad price. Called him up this afternoon and put some pressure on him. He's already transferred me the difference to make it fair, so that's next month's repayment sorted. In the meantime, I'm going to take your advice about getting a lawyer. We've been looking on the internet, not that I understand it much. There are lawyers who do something called '*no win, no fee*'. Luke might be gone, but like you said, his company still exists, so it's worth a shot."

"It certainly is," Julia said as she took Casper into a hug. "It was really nice to meet you."

"You too," Casper said, patting Julia heartily on the back with his free arm. "You're a diamond, like my Heather. Women like you don't come along that often. The sooner Barker puts a ring on your finger, the better!"

Julia instinctively touched her ring finger as her cheeks blushed. She hugged Heather, who dropped the bags to squeeze Julia tightly.

"I'm sorry you got tangled up in our family drama," she whispered into Julia's ear. "There were more skeletons than any of us could have ever imagined."

"We've all got them," Julia said as she pulled away from the hug. "You're both more than welcome in Peridale any time you want a change of scenery."

"You'd have us back?" Casper cried as he hobbled past her. "You really *are* a saint, Julia South. We might take you up on that offer one day."

Heather smiled her goodbyes before following

her husband. Jessie held the door open for the two of them, closing it carefully behind them when they were gone.

"And they were the normal ones," Jessie said with a roll of her eyes. "Sweet, I guess."

They followed the chatter into the sitting room, where Dawn was sitting across from Conrad and Bella. The young couple was sat on opposite sides of the couch, looking in opposite directions. The moment Dawn saw Julia, she hurried over and hugged her.

"You're okay!" she said as she squeezed Julia tightly. "Thank God you're okay. I was starting to worry."

"I'm fine," Julia said, deciding it was not a good time to bring up the elbow to the side of the head she had taken. "And so is Ethan, by the sounds of it, which is the important thing."

"I visited him first thing this morning," Dawn said as she pulled away, her hair straight and her face delicately made up like it had been when Julia had first met her. "We're getting divorced, but we both agreed it was for the best. Our relationship had become toxic before this, but there was no way we could continue after everything. I'm going to be there for him, and we're going to try and stay friends, but we're parting ways. I'm going to pack up my things and stay with my sister for a while until I get on my feet. I still have my job, and I have some exciting building design projects coming up, so that's what I'm going to focus on."

"I'm glad it's going great for *someone*," Conrad mumbled, his face pale and his eyes tired. "All of my big sponsorships have dropped me! Apparently, it doesn't reflect well on them that I *'lied'* about being held hostage, especially after the police denied the report. *#ConradIsOver* was trending this morning, and I've already lost thirty thousand followers!"

"*Jesus Christ!*" Bella muttered, rolling her eyes heavily from behind her hair. "Maybe get a real job, Conrad? People have died, and my dad – my dad *isn't* the man I *thought* he was, and now he's going to ruin my chances of becoming a police officer."

"Why?" Jessie asked, folding her arms as she stared down her nose at Bella. "That's not fair."

"I've read things online that say I probably won't be accepted if my father is a convicted murderer," she said, pulling her phone from her pocket. "I've deleted all of my social apps, though. I'm not going back to that life. I'll stay with my mum for a while and figure out my next move. Maybe I'll go on a gap year? Travel the world and find my place in it."

"That sounds fun," Conrad mumbled as he picked at his nails. "Will be good for taking pictures for content."

Bella huffed as she stood up, casting one final look at Conrad. To Julia's surprise, she pulled her into a hug, and then moved onto Jessie.

"Thank you," she said as she squeezed Jessie, who could not have looked more uncomfortable if she tried. "You made me realise that I didn't have to be that girl anymore. I'll never be able to repay you. I should go. My train is setting off soon. Good luck with Billy. He's one of the good ones."

With one last smile, Bella tucked her brown and blonde hair behind her ears, grabbed her bag from the foot of the stairs, and left the manor.

"So, everyone has a plan *apart* from me?" Conrad wailed as he slammed himself into the couch. "My life is *ruined!*"

"You're a good looking boy," Dawn said as she checked her phone. "You'll land on your feet. Guys like you always do. My taxi is here. Better not keep them waiting." Dawn walked over and patted Julia on the shoulder. "Welcome to the family, Julia. Maybe I'll get an invite to the next family party, maybe I won't. Either way, let's hope it's less like this one, right?"

Julia nodded her agreement, smiling as Dawn grabbed her bag on her way to the door.

"She's pretty calm considering her son is dead, her marriage has broken down, and her fancy piece is a murderer," Jessie said as she stared at the front door. "Maybe she's insane?"

"She's coping," Julia said, understanding the look on Dawn's face all too well. "She's putting on a brave face, so she doesn't have a breakdown. I suspect she'll be a very different woman when she gets home, but she'll get better with time."

Leaving Conrad to contemplate his future in the sitting room, Julia and Jessie headed upstairs. So much had happened in the manor, Julia knew it would never feel the same again.

"Did you and Billy come to a solution?" Julia asked as they walked towards the master bedroom, suddenly remembering seeing them holding hands in the middle of the chaos last night. "Or should I not ask?"

"That's what I wanted to tell you before your phone died last night," Jessie said. "He's staying in Peridale. He said he only wanted to join the army because he thought he had to be a man for everyone. I told him it was okay to be a seventeen-year-old for now. I'm sure a job will come up soon."

"I'm sure it will," Julia said with a nod, the 'HELP WANTED' sign stuck to the door of her father's antique barn springing to the front of her mind. "Life has a funny way of sorting itself out."

"I think I love him," Jessie mumbled, her nostrils flaring as though she had not meant to be so frank. "If you repeat that, I'll kill you."

"My lips are sealed," Julia said, pulling a zip across her mouth and locking it at the corner. "There's been more than enough death around here recently."

After knocking softly on the door, they walked into the dimly lit bedroom. Katie was sitting up in bed with Vinnie sleeping on her chest. Vincent was in his wheelchair next to the bed, his hand limply holding his daughter's, his eyes trained on his first grandson. Dot, Sue, and Barker were crowded around the bottom of the bed, and Brian was next to Katie, staring at the baby as though he had already completely fallen in love with his new son.

"I was wondering when you'd get here," Barker said, pulling Julia into his side. "Have they all gone?"

"Your family?" Julia asked, transfixed by the little baby like everyone else in the room. "They've gone."

"Then we can get back to normal," Barker said, resting his head on top of Julia's as he let out a long sigh. "I have all the family I need in this room right here."

Julia could not have agreed more. She looked at Katie and Brian, finally feeling at ease with their marriage. The similar looks on Dot and Sue's faces let her know they were feeling the same. Julia pulled Jessie into their hug and kissed her on the top of her head, glancing out of the window as faint flakes of snow began to drift from the chalky sky.

"Me too, Barker," Julia said as Jessie wriggled away, flattening her dark hair with a scowl. "*Me too.*"

If you enjoyed *Birthday Cake and Bodies*, why not sign up to Agatha Frost's **free** newsletter at **AgathaFrost.com** to hear about brand new releases!

Coming December 2017! Julia and friends are back for another Peridale Cafe Mystery case in *Gingerbread and Ghosts!*

74753580R00151

Made in the USA
Middletown, DE
30 May 2018